Before Sister
... in Hilltown

by

Wade Gilley

Published by
The John Deaver Drinko Academy
Marshall University, Huntington, West Virginia
and
TRAFFORD

© Copyright 2002 Wade Gilley. All rights reserved.

No part of this publication may be reproduced, stored in a retrieval system, or transmitted, in any form or by any means, electronic, mechanical, photocopying, recording, or otherwise, without the written prior permission of the author.

Printed in Victoria, Canada

National Library of Canada Cataloguing in Publication Data

Gilley, J. Wade
    Before sister / Wade Gilley.
ISBN 1-55395-141-7
    I. Title.
PS3607.I44B43 2002   813'.6   C2002-904639-4

TRAFFORD

This book was published *on-demand* in cooperation with Trafford Publishing.
On-demand publishing is a unique process and service of making a book available for retail sale to the public taking advantage of on-demand manufacturing and Internet marketing. **On-demand publishing** includes promotions, retail sales, manufacturing, order fulfilment, accounting and collecting royalties on behalf of the author.

Suite 6E, 2333 Government St., Victoria, B.C. V8T 4P4, CANADA
Phone   250-383-6864   Toll-free   1-888-232-4444 (Canada & US)
Fax   250-383-6804   E-mail   sales@trafford.com
Web site www.trafford.com   TRAFFORD PUBLISHING IS A DIVISION OF TRAFFORD HOLDINGS LTD.
Trafford Catalogue #02-0855   www.trafford.com/robots/02-0855.html

10   9   8   7   6   5   4   3   2

Author's Note

The stories of Before Sister are all essentially true as are most of the names and nicknames used in the book. On occasions two or more stories have been merged into one to better tell the tale of Momma and the Hilltown community. I have used pseudonyms for some people, and on other occasions have combined two or more personalities into one for clarification and simplification. I have also taken certain liberties with the telling of some stories, particularly with the precise sequence of events and who may have said what to whom. My intention in allowing the narrative to stray from strict nonfiction was always to provide more insight. It must be remembered that many of the details in the stories of happenings before I started school, and afterwards, have been etched in my memory by a continuous retelling of these stories by my Daddy and Momma—and others. In other words they are a confluence of the memories of more than one person. It is also important to note that Hilltown like most communities had a more dire side than is presented here. (It had a more glorious side too.) My mother, my father and my relatives were not perfect as no human is or ever will be. There are many Hilltown and Fries stories which have been not been dealt with here but might be told in later efforts. All in all these communities were good, if not perfect, places for a young boy to grow up in the 1940s and 1950s.

Wade Gilley

Acknowledgements

The statement that no man is an island is true when an engineer sits down to write a novel, fiction or nonfiction. That was certainly true of this book. **Before Sister**... *in Hilltown.*

There are many to thank and acknowledge.

First, there is my steadfast wife of forty years Nanna, our daughter Cheryl, and my sister Mickey for their persistent encouragement, challenging of facts and serious editing from time to time. My son, Wade, Jr., for his brotherhood, and to my Daddy, Woodrow "Big Stick" Gilley, for his encouragement, challenges and support over more than fifty years.

To the folks at Marshall University, who have meant so much to me; C. T Mitchell, for his editorial expertise, Bob Hayes, Alan Gould and others who know the Appalachian Mountain people so well and are in the encouragement business a heartfelt thanks for their interest and support.

To Jessica Andersen a special thanks for wise counsel and editorial assistance.

To my Aunt Belle and her daughter Toodie Blevins, descendants of Oda, for their interest and willingness to help. To my high school mates Harold Mitchell and Ken Lanter for their active interest and encouragement.

To my good friends Drs. John Deaver and Elizabeth Drinko for their support and encouragement over the years and in this specific case for supporting the writing and publishing of this book. I hope to express my appreciation to the Drinkos in a more tangible way—sometime.

And finally to **Momma** who took a tow-headed, overly active mountain boy showed him a way, gave him a start and offered critical support and guidance so often when it was needed. This book has been in the making for so many years and it is my way of saying thanks to Momma.

Momma it is your story.

Table of Contents

I'm Momma! 9
Prologue 15
Who Is He? 20
Momma 27
Home Alone with Momma 40
    No Momma I'm not Running Away! 40
    Rushing to the Lewis Gayle 43
    The China Cabinet Falls. 48
    Hurrying, I Lose My Front Teeth 52
    No Hangings Allowed Around Here 57
Time of Growing Up 62
    The Wholesale House 62
    Queenie, My Queenie 76
    Going 'Coon Huntin' 82
ODA: A Mother, A Grandmother 89
    Lye Soap and Soap Operas 90
    Kidnapping Rube and Reba Marries 96
    ODA's Way 103
    Oh No Not Russ! 108
Momma Gets Her Wishes 114
Growing-Up Pains 120
    The Best Five Dollars Ever Spent 120
    Hobnobbing with the Splendid Splinter 129
    After Hobnobbing - The New River. 135
    Juvenile Delinquent, Almost 140
    A Summer of Fear and Adventure 150
What Do You Want to Be? 160
Epilogue 171
Appendix 175
    Fries! 175

I'm Momma!

Many folks in my hometown of Hilltown had descriptive nicknames, as was common in the southern Appalachian Mountains. There was a gender difference, however. The nicknames of men and boys were used everywhere, but the nicknames of the women and girls generally weren't used in public unless that name was so descriptive or flattering as to be used universally.

My grandfather, Alex—or Alec—Hill, was known by everyone as *Windy*. His brothers were *Possum, Snotty, Shorty* and *Hound Dog,* all names descriptive of the person's nose, stature or favorite pastime. These were usually earned at an early age and stuck until death. However, only one of their seven sisters had a nickname that I knew—Florence Hill Carico was called *Huldy*, after her penny-pinching ways.

My daddy, Woodrow Charles Gilley, came to Hilltown in his mid-20s and gained the nicknames *Woody* for Woodrow, or *Big Stick*, which he earned during his years as an officer at the Radford Ammunition Plant. He was called *Big Gilley* by some because at six-foot-five and more than two hundred fifty pounds, he wasn't a small man by Hilltown standards. That name came to haunt me in later years when I, the six-foot-two, two hundred thirty pound captain of the Fries High School Wildcats football team, was referred to as *Little Gilley*.

I escaped that nickname when I went on to college and off into the world of work, but I did hear it one other time in later years. One night when my son was in the ninth grade, the phone rang and I answered to hear a young female voice say, "Wade is that you?"

I responded, "Which Wade are you looking for?"

She paused for a minute and then stuttered, "Why the big one," meaning my son, who had inherited his grandfather's frame. For that moment I was *Little Gilley* again.

However that had been my second nickname. I earned the first when I was just two years old and fascinated by my parents' strawberry patch. My appetite for the luscious berries became well known in that end of Hilltown and someone, probably Daddy, gave me the name *Hawberry* or Awberry—my way of pronouncing strawberry.

There was an obvious reason for some nicknames, but not always. Florence was *Huldy* for her frugal ways, but her husband, Leff Carico—also known for his parsimony—had no nickname as far as I know. Her brother Kelvy was commonly known as *Possum* for the length of his nose, according to my daddy. Huldy had another brother called *Shorty*. This one puzzled me since all the Hills were very short. So why was one named Shorty—unless it a was a reference to something other than his height? To my knowledge none of *Huldy's* sisters had nicknames even though several of her aunts, born in the 1870s or so, did

Huldy's sister Bell married a man named Edgar Funk from up in Grayson County's Spring Valley, and they moved to a tract out on the west end of Hilltown Road. Ed had his own nickname, earned in midlife when he became a taxi owner/driver. The Scots-Irish men of Hilltown dug deep into their roots to name him *Jitney*, Scottish for taxi cab.

Leff and *Huldy's* adopted son, William Carico, earned his own name when he came down Hilltown Road sometime in the early 1930s to report that Leff had bought a new Chevrolet sedan. The ruling fathers of Hilltown noted that he announced his daddy had bought a *"She-Dan"* and that became his name for the rest of his time in the community.

Other nicknames were much like those in any southern or mountain community. For example:

Wormy was for those who looked sickly as youngsters, suggesting they had a case of worms.

Knotty had bumps on his head from some parasite or nutritional factor.

They said *Dirty* loved to play in the mud.

Booger was known for picking his nose.

There were two *Mooses* and it's possible that their lumbering gaits were the source of their names, even though both were athletes of a sort.

Sap was just that, I suppose.

In Fries High School we had a Gary *Gobby* or *Gabby* Farmer who could—or tried to—talk fast.

C'nt (sorry ladies) was the unlucky cousin who got caught in the back of a car undressed with his 15-year-old girlfriend (and distant cousin) and served 18 months for statutory rape.

Birddog had his favorite sport and was content with his name.

Baldy was... at the tender age of twenty, which was more common than not among the Hills.

Gander was a good looking little girl and a first cousin of mine.

Doad just lounged around home most of the time. He might as well have been dead.

Fotch once attempted to use fancier talk than the community was accustomed to, only to be caught and reminded of his mistake forever.

And *Botch* just couldn't get things straight.

Billy *Sheriff* Wingate's father was in law enforcement.

For good reason, Randell King became known as *Sideburns* when that hairstyle made a comeback in the late 1950s.

My cousin and classmate at Fries High was Ruth *Flame* Crowder for her flaming red hair. And one of the football stars just ahead of me in school was Harry *Red* Patton for the same reason.

Ed Creagar weighed about 300 pounds and was, of course, *Big Ed*.

Big Ed's companion in the middle of the Wildcat defensive line was Tony *Two Ton* Burdette, also a 300 pounder.

One of the boys from over Ivanhoe way was *Hotdog*, while my cousin, Travis Hill, was *Tab*—and that was unrelated to the soft drink, which came along some years later.

Swanson Burcham was *Cotton* for his boyish white hair.

And my buddy, Harold Mitchell, was *Mitch* as has been the case with all the Mitchells I've encountered.

I recall only one other girl in my graduating class at Fries who had a nickname—tomboyish Jane *Lefty* Davis.

I never understood why our neighbor and cousin by marriage, *Screwball* Smith, got his name. He was so knowledgeable about animals that veterinarians would leave certain medicines with him to administer in routine cases. He helped my mother and sister in the troublesome delivery of a calf at one point. Perhaps he was so intelligent that his thinking was on a different plane just not understood in Hilltown, so they dismissed him.

Ne-nee wet his pants as a two-year-old and cried, "ne-nee, ne-nee" when he couldn't have his way.

T-wan was, of course, the one who placed golf balls on tees for company bosses using the outfield at the Fries ballpark for a driving range. Or maybe, as some said, he thought he was "*The Wan.*"

We had one cousin named *Little Roy* or *Spec* Hill. His father was Roy but why *Spec* I don't know.

There were several *Juniors* around and they were named for their fathers—or some thought that they should be so named.

Junebug and *Firefly* were named for their early pursuit of those fascinating, hard-to-catch creatures. Though both were talented, they never seemed to catch their dreams.

Names such as *Mattie* or *Hattie* or *Katie or Nattie* came as abbreviations of more formal names and did not reflect any character trait or misstep. But *Katie My Lady* for Kaitlyn might say something special about a girl.

I played some football with *Pooky* Farmer who went onto be a star at the Virginia Military Institute.

Windy Hill's three boys (uncles of mine) all had nicknames. The youngest, Homer, loved to whistle and was affectionately known as *Whis* while the next older, Horace, was called *G'burn* after he married his very religious third wife, Bertha, who wouldn't put up with curse words. The oldest brother was known as *P'toke*—neither an affectionate name nor a terribly descriptive one. He was just *P'toke*.

Among the cousins there was Lawrence *Dollar* Hill who was a serious businessman, automobile mechanic, painter and someone who knew the value of a dollar. *Dollar* or *Dollar Bill* as some called him refrained from giving free help to the dozens of cousins and uncles who would have liked to have him work on their cars—for free, of course.

Stringbean and *Stick* were usually used in reference to skinny body structures while *Gas* in one case referenced a bodily function—at times uncontrollable.

Sonny was usually preferable to a birth name such as Clive or perhaps represented an only son—respectfully referenced as such.

Boomie or *Boomer* was the nickname of a successful—at the college level—baseball player who, ironically, was a pitcher.

Hav'it was the summer league outfielder who pursuing a pop fly kept yelling, "I hav'it, I hav'it, I hav'it" until the baseball slipped through his outstretched hands and hit him in the forehead—causing the delay of an important game.

One of my first cousins, Louise's boy, her first, was a scrappy fellow who became a state policeman in North Carolina and retired with his nickname of *Scrappy* still intact.

One cousin had three car wrecks before he was 21, leaving the guys around the old coal stove at the Jot 'em Down store wondering how he avoided more, was *Crash*, of course.

Our cousin and *P'toke's* eldest son, Kenneth Hill, was called *Bice* because he was always talking about being the *bice* or boss. It seemed that more than anything else he wanted to be in charge of something.

Without those names, life growing up in the southern Appalachian Mountains would have been a lot less colorful.

I first learned about nicknames one Sunday afternoon sitting on the front porch listening to Momma talk to a truck driver.

"Thanks Forest, I'll talk to Alec Hill about this," the man said getting into his pickup truck to drive down the dirt road to Grandpa Windy's house.

I turned to Momma who was sitting on the porch swing reading to me, "Momma why did he call Grandpa Windy 'Alec'?"

"That's his given name," she retorted in a matter of fact way.
"What's a given name?"

Impatient to get on with reading *Gone with the Wind* out loud (again) Momma answered, "Everyone has a family name and then a given name. Your family name is Gilley and your given name is Wade. Do you understand?"

"But why is Grandpa called Windy? Is that his given name? Does he have two given names?"

"No, Windy is his nickname. Everybody has a given name and then a nickname,"

"Oh, so Wade is my given name?"

"Yes Wade, and you're Awberry too, your Daddy said so."

"So why is grandpa called Windy?"

"Because he likes to talk so much, that's why," she said in a tone indicating that she really wanted to finish that book chapter. "People get their nicknames when they earn them."

"You said everybody has a nickname. But you don't," I continued. "Everybody calls you Forest."

A twinkle came in her eyes and she said, half smiling, "I have a nickname all right, and it's the most special nickname of all."

I perked up, interested. "You do? What is it?"

She smiled and hugged me. "I'm Momma."

Prologue

The Call…

"Wish we'd talked more," Momma said in the weakest voice I'd ever heard from her. Come to think of it, I didn't think I'd ever heard definitive, down to earth Momma wish either. This was so… unlike her. She continued, "Wade, we need to talk."

"I know, I know, Momma. It seems like the world is going by in a flash. The kids are growing up so fast," I replied. "We're coming home to see you this weekend and you and I can talk then." *We need to take the kids to visit Momma more*, I thought to myself. She was back in the hospital after surviving breast cancer surgery five years earlier, and though we'd visited as often as possible, it never felt like enough.

"Wish we could talk like we did when we lived in Roanoke," Momma whispered, and I knew her mind was traveling back to the second-level flat in Roanoke, Virginia where we'd lived for a while during World War II. I'd been five years old and Daddy had been working as a train engineer on long War Department hauls. Momma and I spent practically every minute of every day together, even huddling beside each other to sleep. We'd been inseparable.

Attempting to change the subject, I asked, "How are you feeling, Momma? How is the Roanoke Memorial Hospital treating you?"

"I had a treatment again today. Made me sick," she responded, and then changed the subject back to what was on her mind. "Do you remember going to the park and feeding the squirrels?"

"Yes, Momma," I said. "They always seemed to know that you had peanuts in that paper bag the way they came running and jumping all over both of us before we could sit down." *Why was Momma thinking of things forty years in the past?* I thought. Momma was always the person who looked ahead and planned for the future. She didn't look back.

A niggling suspicion formed in my head. "Has Sister been to visit you today?"

"She went home," Momma whispered

I shook my head, thinking, *Thank God for Sister. While I've been running like a gerbil on a wheel she stays close to home. What a support she's been for Momma and Daddy.* I said, "Momma, you rest now. We'll drive out to see you tonight. Is that okay?"

"When we lived in Roanoke we talked all the time. Just us. Do you remember?" Her voice seemed, if possible, a little fainter.

I nodded, though she couldn't see me over the phone. "We didn't have anyone else. Daddy was away and there were no Hilltown folks around. It was just the two of us."

"You could read the *Roanoke Times*," she quavered proudly. "Could have gone to school that year but, they wouldn't let you."

"I remember. You taught me to read. But that didn't matter to the schools. They lived by rules." I glanced at my watch and realized I was late for a meeting. I explained this to Momma and reminded her that my wife Nanna, the kids and I would drive out to see her tonight.

Shortly, an obviously tired Momma said, "I've wanted to talk for a long time."

Then she hung up. I later realized that was her way of saying goodbye.

Sitting in my office, gazing out the window at nothing and clutching the telephone to my chest, I didn't want to accept the sense of loneliness that crept over me. It had been one year to the day since we lost our first daughter and now Momma wasn't sounding so good.

Quickly packing my briefcase I (the scheduled meeting fading in importance) left the office for the Fourth of July weekend to drive home and pick up the family. We were packed and ready to leave for the trip when Sister called. "Wade," she said in a halting and husky voice, "Wade, she's gone."

Why didn't I take the time to talk to her more? What was so important that I couldn't find time? Why didn't I find time? Why? Why? I found myself thinking as I said something reassuring to Sister and hung up the phone.

We rode up Interstate 81, and the kids soon fell asleep in the back of the station wagon. For a while my wife and I talked about the arrangements that we'd need to make. "It was just a year ago today that Momma stood with us as we buried Dennie," I remembered. "Now we're going to place Momma beside her."

Nanna placed her hand on my knee while the mile markers passed in a series of green-white blurs. "She loved all her grandbabies."

In the quietness of the night, my thoughts drifted back to the early years of my childhood when we'd lived in Roanoke. It had been Momma's idea to move from our home in Hilltown to the small apartment in Roanoke. "We'll have more time with Daddy," she'd said. With Daddy working long hours and spending several nights a week away from home, it was just Momma and me, a one on one, day and night existence. Each day she read the *Roanoke Times* front to back as I sat and listened. It was part of her frantic wartime effort to teach me so many things, to assure that I was ready to begin school.

As the car rolled through the night, memories of her flooded back like a dam bursting.

"Wade, Wade, get up. It's time to go to the beach." Her hands had shaken me awake. It was the day Momma had made arrangements for the two of us to ride the train from Roanoke to Norfolk and then to Ocean View for a day at the beach. I was just over four years old.

"It's dark outside," I sleepily replied rubbing my eyes. Who wanted to get up at two o'clock in the morning, drive to the train station and take the train all night just to go to the ocean and see the beach? Nobody I knew ever went to the beach, at least no one from Hilltown.

"You said you'd go when we talked about it and you're going to have that day at the beach," she replied. "We're going." There was no pulling back after committing to Momma, even if it meant a 23-hour round trip on the train for a few hours at the beach and the amusement park. Over the years, this trip had loomed ever larger in my memories. It had been a long, long day full of exciting memories: the train, trolleys, my first cotton candy, the huge white beach and the limitless ocean had all seemed very large. As usual, Momma had given her young son from the Blue Ridge Mountains something very special to remember.

Once on a car trip to North Carolina, I remember telling Momma that I was bored. "How long before we get to see the Indians? How long?" I'd queried from the back seat of our car. She had decided that we needed to go to North Carolina to see the Cherokees.

"Do you know you've got three grandmothers who were part Cherokee?"

She glanced over at Daddy who was concentrating on the crooked roads and smoking his Camel. She then pulled a book from her handbag. I crawled over into the front seat to sit in her lap as she read a fictional story about the Cherokees and their life in North Carolina. From that long car trip I gained a lifelong memory of distant relatives and a whole other living environment. It wasn't like Hilltown.

Another time she told Mrs. Jackson, my second grade teacher, on the first day of school, "Give him a paddling whenever he needs it and send a note home and I'll give him another one." Momma meant for me to get the most out of school. It was due to her that I went on to become a teacher, a college president and a secretary of education.

Another time when I was older she gave me her hand written grocery list and said, "Here's ten dollars and seventy five cents, you buy everything on this list and you can keep any leftover money." Frugal Momma knew how to get a job done while at the same time teaching me a lesson on money management. I am sure she felt it was needed, as Daddy had just gone bankrupt and we had lost our two cars and one hauling truck. I became Momma's delegated grocery shopper with Granny Oda on Saturday mornings. It was a well-learned lesson in Scots-Irish thriftiness, one my children often accused me of learning too well.

Momma was always teaching me something one way or another, and those lessons made me the man I became.

In those early years, it was all teaching and learning. Momma had dropped out of school at fifteen to work ten hours a day six days a week in the cotton mill, but she never quit learning. She was unique in her time and place. She was a talented homemaker, wife and mother. She went to work when most women stayed home, and became the first woman in Hilltown to own a car and travel to distant places.

Momma believed in hard work *and education* as a sure path to a better future, and as I drove across the state to bury her, I realized that she'd tried to use our last conversation on this earth to offer me one more lesson. She wanted me to stop and smell the roses, to take time to talk to my children. She also wanted me to know that a mother's love is constant, no matter that it is changed by time, by distance, or by the addition of new family members.

Because of this lesson, I would like to tell you a story.

It is the story of Forest Gladys Hill Gilley from Hilltown, Virginia. It is a story of a woman who was shaped by her time and her town as much as she broke from its expectations, and whose greatest goal in life was to see her son and daughter end up better educated than she ever was. And it is a story of a relationship that changes—but never dies.

Who Is He?

One of my first memories of Forest Gladys Hill Gilley, my Momma, is of a Sunday morning in 1941 when she excitedly (and she could get excited!) came hustling up the steep concrete front steps to our house in Hilltown and told me to get ready. "We're going with Grandpa to Huldy's for Sunday dinner. You'll get to see Grandmother Martha Jane!" She meant her grandmother (my great grandmother), and because Momma was excited, I, too, became excited.

"Martha Jane?" I asked

"Martha Jane is Martha Jane, you'll see," she retorted hustling as the screen door banged shut. She had to fix a dish on short notice.

Grandma Martha Jane was a legend of sorts but I hadn't yet met her in my four years on earth.

Martha Jane had co-founded Hilltown, and to my childish eyes looked ancient. She was 94 that year. Martha Jane never reached 95, and that Sunday was special to Momma because she felt a bond with her grandmother that she'd lacked with her own mother.

Martha Jane Corvin Hill, born in 1847 in Wythe County, Virginia to Joseph Corvin and his second wife Elizabeth Kriegger, was a late arrival in the 23 child family. Martha was an unexpected blessing for the Corvin family, and hadn't been included in her father's will. Rather than pay lawyers to rewrite the will, Joseph made arrangements to give her a small lot in the county seat of Wytheville as her inheritance. That plot of ground is where the Wythe County Courthouse now stands and has for some one hundred years.

When Martha Jane married John R. Hill in 1867, the land gave the young couple the opportunity to trade for several hundred acres of elevated rolling plateau at the great bend of the ancient New River where it crossed the border of Grayson and Carroll counties in Virginia. The Blue Ridge Mountain area is just east of Bartlett Falls in Grayson County, where the town of Fries was built in 1901 in conjunction with the construction of a major hydroelectric dam and a cotton mill, all authorized by an act of Congress.

In this beautiful, untamed part of the Virginia hills, John and Martha built a log cabin, set up housekeeping, began farming and reared their 12 children. As the children grew to adulthood, the parents gave parcels of land to several—usually the boys but sometimes to the girls if they needed the help. This division of land made it impossible for any one of their children to make a living farming, but it did lead to creation of a Hill family community which became known in due time as Hilltown.

The second generation of Hills, including my grandfather, Alex "Windy" Hill and his wife Flora Jane Harrison, who inherited John and Martha's home and were in turn determined to provide homesteads of sorts for their male children where possible—right nearby. Thus, by 1942 Hilltown encompassed a two-mile stretch of dirt and gravel road from the town limits of Fries to the south all the way to U. S. Route 94 at Hawkstown. It was home to more than three-dozen families and some 200 souls, all related through the Hills.

I grew up in this elevated mountainous country community, cheek by jowl acquainted with more than 60 of my cousins. Everyone knew everything about everybody in Hilltown. There was no place to hide.

It was a unique time and a unique place; and it was filled with unique people including Forest Gladys Hill, the fifth child of Alex and Flora Jane Hill, and my Momma.

This is our story.

Each week in those days of the late 1930s and early 1940s, one of Martha Jane's children would cook Sunday dinner for her at her home, which she shared with her daughter, Florence "Huldy"

Hill Carico, Huldy's husband Leff and their several adopted children. On this particular Sunday it was my grandfather Alex "Windy" Hill's turn to host Sunday dinner and he, like his siblings, brought as many of his clan as could be rounded up for the occasion. Thus, Grandpa Windy and Flora Jane, plus my mother, several of her siblings and a dozen or more of Martha's great grandchildren were going for Sunday dinner with this special lady. (In Hilltown in those days, dinner was the full noonday meal—not to be confused with supper, which was the evening meal.)

It was a grand opportunity for me as a four-year-old to play hide and seek and cowboys and Indians with several cousins and to see the long dinner table laid out with what could only be described as a feast. I vividly remember Grandpa Windy bringing a full plate of roast beef to place at the center of the dining room table on that Sunday. Roast beef was a rarity in those years. Most of our meat came from pork, chicken and a variety of wild animals including squirrel and rabbit.

My cousins and I had a wonderful time that day racing around and through, in and out of Huldy's house, which was the largest and best furnished home in all Hilltown. By some means never clear to me, she and Leff had secured a hundred-acre farm that included access to the New River. They operated a ferry over the river for those in this isolated section of Carroll County who wanted to go south to the county seat of Hillsville or on to North Carolina. It was whispered that Leff and Huldy had made a fortune with the ferry and were "rich." Who knows, and what is rich? I didn't understand rich then and I know now it is a very relative term.

Leff and Huldy were not as well known for their sociability as they were for their parsimony and I am certain that while Huldy appreciated the support from her brothers and sisters, it was difficult to endure 20 or so of Windy's clan, even if he did provide the food for dinner. But to us kids, Huldy's farmhouse was like a castle—so large, so many rooms… so mysterious….

The house faced west toward the focal ridge and the main thoroughfare, Hilltown Road. The large garden and vineyard to the south stood between the house and the outbuildings, which in-

Wiley Hill, son of John Robert and Martha Hill, with family dog in Hilltown in the 1930s.

cluded one of the largest barns that part of Virginia had ever seen. I later learned that the barn contained "Leff's suite"—a small bedroom with a closet that Leff had built, according to Hilltown gossip, for those times when he and Huldy were not on speaking terms.

Leff was a hard worker, which was apparent from the immaculate condition of his farm—and from the accounts of his money-making skills. As a young man he had traveled west to Nebraska and other Great Plains states working as a transient farm laborer in the wheat fields. Then he ran that ferry for years, only quitting when U. S. 58 was built over the New River, connecting our world to the 5,000 person city of Galax and the county seat Hillsville. It was said that Leff brought home every penny he earned—and lots more, whatever that meant.

Their success was assured when he married Huldy, who'd earned her nickname because she was so frugal. Folks in Hilltown earned their nicknames, which usually described or defined that person in some unique way. Your nickname was given for a lifetime, and to this day I do not know the birth names of some Hilltown men—only their nicknames. And while men were almost always referred to by their nicknames, even in public, it was considered in bad taste to refer to a woman by hers—unless it had become so apparent and common as to conquer tradition.

Huldy had earned her nickname so convincingly that it was used routinely—even to her face. The word 'Huldy', in Hilltown terms meant a stinginess not called for in that community. Though she and Leff were perhaps the most prosperous couple in all Hilltown, Huldy continued her practice of sitting on her screened porch during early fall evenings clawing the juicy hulls off black of walnuts. She saved the walnuts for cracking and to be used in delicious desserts during the winter months. The black walnut juice from the not-quite-dry hulls would leave her hands stained dark brown for weeks. Usually grown ups would have the children take the hull off the walnuts, but not Aunt Florence. She didn't want anything wasted, and the walnuts were better when the hulls were still fresh and juicy. Thus, she became known for the rest of her life as Huldy simply because she had earned it. She would do the dirty work herself if it saved money.

This particular Sunday, my cousins and I took charge of Huldy's house—much to her chagrin I am sure.

Cousins Ne-nee and Tab and I were racing in, around and through her house. We would enter the large side porch, dash through the sitting room, through the living room to the front of the house and burst out the screen door, off the porch and into the yard. As usual, being the youngest and a follower, I was last.

Once, in a wild dash that would never be tolerated on a normal day, I popped out of the front screen door and stopped dead in my tracks. And stared. It was as though I was in a trance. There she was, 94 year-old Martha Jane. She was sitting in her blue Sunday dress, leaning slightly back in the large rocking chair with her head on a pillow, her long (waist length, it was said) white hair neatly wrapped in a bun at the nape of her neck. She was receiving the intense attention of Windy, my daddy and the other men. Momma and the other women were inside preparing Sunday dinner, which would be served in the early afternoon.

There she was—the grand dame, the founder of Hilltown—my great grandmother who had lived through the Civil War, the Spanish-American War, and World War I and now the beginning of World War II. Her image that afternoon has remained forever fixed in my mind. I stood in awe, which wasn't easy for an active four year-old boy. But there are some things and places that demand that one just stop dead—like the entrance to the U. S. Supreme Court where an impressive statute of John Marshall sits, or a formal courtroom, or I suspect an audience with Queen Elizabeth or Queen Victoria. Martha Jane's very presence seemed to demand attention and deference. And it didn't hurt that Daddy and Grandpa Windy, men to whom I deferred (usually) were standing beside her with their hats in their hands.

As I stood there, Martha Jane turned her head, leaned her slim, fragile body forward and looked directly at me through amazingly vivid blue grey eyes. I was frozen in place by those bright eyes. She stared at me forever or so it seemed.

Then in a quiet but clear voice she dominated the gathering, everybody stood at attention when she asked, "Who is he?"

"Who is he?" Those were words I shall never forget because I've asked them of myself at various times over the years.

Who was I anyway? No one had ever asked that before.

"He's Forest's boy," Grandpa Windy stepped forward and said.

"Forest's boy?" She repeated.

"Forest's and Woodrow's boy," Grandpa Windy corrected himself.

"Forest's boy," she repeated again looking directly into my eyes. Then she said, "Boy, you take care to mind your Momma. She will do you good." She paused. "Forest is a doer."

But what I heard was, *Forest's boy.*

Grandpa was right about that and Martha Jane was right about Momma. She was a doer. I was then and always would be Forest's boy. That was a fact of birth and a function of Momma's intense and uncompromising devotion to me and my future during those formative years.

She was my Momma, and I was her boy.

Momma

Forest Gladys Hill was born in Hilltown in October of 1913 at Windy and Flora Jane's house on Hilltown Road, overlooking the holler where Martha and John had settled in late 1869. Momma was the fifth of ten children.

Alex "Windy" Hill and his bride, Flora Jane Harrison of Carroll County by way of East Tennessee and reputed to be of Cherokee decent, had secured some 30 acres of land from John R. and Martha Jane and established their homestead on a ridge with a magnificent view of the upper New River highlands. You could stand on their front porch and see a long stretch of the New River as it flowed into Virginia from the Appalachian highlands of North Carolina.

The original houses in Hilltown were all built at or near freshwater springs but the advent of the Industrial Age made drilling deep water wells possible, which led to settlements along the ridge tops and gave Hilltown longer term growth potential. The number of houses was no longer dependent on the number of springs.

The particular frame and clapboard house belonging to Alex and Flora Jane was built along the new gravelly Hilltown Road on a little knoll about 30 feet above the road. Their barn, garage and woodshed—where a wagon, or later an automobile could be sheltered—were all in one weathered wooden building on the lower side of the road where the hillside sloped steeply. It was behind that barn that six year-old Ne-nee and I once stoned an angry black snake to death before it could slither under the foundation, only to have Grandpa Windy say, "Those copperheads are dangerous." That was scary; everyone knew how dangerous copperheads

Forest Gladys Hill in 1930 at age 17.

were and that you didn't fool with them like you could blacksnakes. In Hilltown, experience was considered an opportunity to teach a lesson and Grandpa Windy never passed up an opportunity.

At the bottom of the slope ran the branch—small stream of water—that was born in the freshwater spring that Martha Jane had used. I caught my first crawdad in that small stream. Looking down that steep hillside to the tiny branch today, it is hard to imagine grazing cows there, but those Hills of Scots-Irish descent found no problem with that.

Windy's house overlooked the site where John and Martha's log cabin had once stood in the holler below, and originally consisted of three rooms—a bedroom, a living/sitting room and an eat-in kitchen. It had three porches—one overlooking the original Hill homestead with a view of the upper New River Valley, a second one looking south toward the great bend of the river and another smaller porch off the kitchen overlooking the smokehouse, the spring house and the orchard.

Windy and Flora Jane (Flora Jane had a nickname but I can't say it in public) added to their family every 24 months or so until they had a total of ten children. Consequently, their house was expanded periodically. A kitchen was added to the north, and a porch was enclosed and became an addition to the kitchen. The south-facing porch was enclosed to provide two bedrooms. By the time my mother left home, the house had seven rooms, an anteroom, two porches, and a dirt-floor room underneath for storing canned goods, cabbage and potatoes, etc. That 1,700 square-foot house, which included formal living and dining rooms, was where Windy and Flora Jane lived their lives and raised their family.

About 400 feet to the north of them was a tract of land owned by Windy's brother, Ellis Hill. Huldy and Leff's farm sat between Ellis' place and the New River. Behind and to the south of Grandpa's farm was his brother Sam's home, which was about 20 acres. All in all, Windy and seven of his eleven brothers and sisters had acquired land from their parents along the dirt road. In doing so, they established the physical and social structure of Hilltown.

Each of those eight children provided land for as many of their own offspring as possible, leading to a community of more than

30 houses and families by the time I was born in 1938. Some 200 people, all related in one way or another, lived in Hilltown and by 1940 were sharing the same telephone party line.

The population of the area never grew dramatically because, unlike the Appalachian Mountain communities that boasted coal fields or heavy industry, Hilltown saw limited immigration. The building of the cotton mill at Bartlett Falls, which led to the founding of Fries, was an exception. But that event had little influence on the demographics of Hilltown, which was controlled by the Hills, including Windy and Flora Jane, who raised my momma.

Amongst the Hill heritage of short Scots-Irish folk, Martha Jane and her granddaughter Forest Gladys had the distinction of being the two tallest people in Hilltown, man or woman. Momma bore the brunt of her family's teasing about being tall, but she chuckled about it when I was a young boy. "No man tall enough for me, huh?"

When she'd married my six-foot-five-inch Daddy, she had "showed them" and was proud of it.

Until Momma came into her full height at age 15, Martha Jane was one of if not the tallest person in Hilltown. She was one of the tallest persons in the 23 child Corvin family, and it was said that she inherited it from her mother Elizabeth Kriegger, Joseph's Corvin's second wife and the mother of the last seventeen of his 23 children. Elizabeth was a tall German woman and passed her height on to Martha Jane who apparently passed it on to Momma, along with her spirited nature and determination.

Momma was tall, slim, and reportedly exuded an aura of 'can do' energy all through her twenties. She excelled in school but had to drop out after sporadic seventh grade attendance, because her parents couldn't afford to send her to Fries High School, which was just a mile away but located in Grayson County, thereby requiring tuition. She had learned to sew and make clothes in that seventh grade class, and used that skill to her and her family's advantage for decades. This was one way she occupied her energetic and fertile mind.

On leaving school, Forest Hill went to work in the Fries cotton mill—10 hours a day, six days a week for $3.50 a week. She lived at home, paid room and board, saw that her mother had the first Frigidaire (the Frigidaire was so dominant in the refrigerator market that everyone owned a "Frigidaire" regardless of its make) in all Hilltown, bought herself an almost-new Chevrolet roadster and a beautiful ankle-length Russian pony fur coat (which my sister owns to this day) and started planning for marriage and housekeeping by laying away china, dinnerware and a full formal dining room suite at the company store in Fries. She also managed to enjoy trips to the beach and other places in and around Virginia between ages 16 and 23. When Forest was 23, she married my father—who was just as energetic and ambitious but less practical in ways dealing with money.

This would be a theme throughout their lives.

They wed on October 16, 1937. I was born on August 15, 1938 and my parents bought their first house, next door to Grandpa Hill and across the road from her brother "P'toke" and his wife Callie and their five children: Billy, Bice, Junebug, Knotty and Gander (the baby and only girl). I was delivered at home by Dr. Cox, the Fries town doctor, and I was virtually inseparable from Momma for the next six years.

During Daddy's absence through the war years, she moved me into her bed where we slept together most nights, except when Daddy was home, until it was almost time for my sister to be born in October of 1945. She must have put me out when her pregnancy began to show.

I was an only child for those first six years, and Momma made me an integral part of her daily life—every hour, every minute. When she got mail she read it to me whether I could understand it or not. When I was 3 or 4 she read me complete stories from the weekly *Grit* (America's national newspaper in those days). When she received a telephone call she explained it to me even when I was a toddler, telling me who called, why, and what was said. Then she frequently would add her own lengthy analysis of the call.

Momma had an opinion on everything and everybody and with me she was very free to express her thoughts

For example, when she drove the 30 miles to Wytheville to

pick up Daddy at the train station, she never left me with a relative even though there were plenty around. This included late night and early morning trips. It didn't matter—we were together. I would usually sit in the passenger side front seat while she talked to me all the way there. She explained scenes, buildings and history that I could not see from my position, much less understand. That never slowed her down or, if it did, I never noticed. In those days there were no seat belts or baby seats so we both bounced around a lot riding over those dirt roads. And the whole while we bounced, we talked.

While most people meeting Forest Hill Gilley the first time would come away thinking that she was reserved, those of us close to her knew Momma was full of herself. She was especially opinionated about people she knew, or that she thought I should know. When it came to using personalities as a point of reference for daily living, she did not hesitate to make a negative lesson—again and again.

But more than anything else, Momma was hungry for knowledge. She literally devoured books, buying some but most often borrowing and exchanging, for even in this passion she was frugal, not unlike Huldy, because times were always tight in Hilltown.

It seemed everybody raised and killed hogs for meat and everybody had a garden. People helped each other kill hogs and pick corn and beans depending on the season. Meat was cured in smoke houses and it seemed everything that wasn't nailed down was canned for future use. This was one way to improve your life without having to have cash and it was something that distinguished the residents of Hilltown. Practically everybody in Hilltown had a little land and made use of it to enhance their standard of living. Some Hills had root cellars where they stored roots and tubers for winter eating. What wouldn't keep in the cellar could be kept in a can. This was part of the culture and a way to make life better in tight times.

But Hilltown was more than a collection of hillbilly houses.

From my own memories and the photographs all of us would sit around and look at from time to time, I know that Hilltown was a different place. There was a 'can do' attitude that I sensed was absent in the deeper South or the emerging Ghettos of the cities during the Great Depression.

In the late 1940s, the men and women of our community dressed in outfits straight out of the Roaring 20s. Men wore Ivy caps, Bowler hats and short brimmed Stetsons or work hats with longer brims. They bowed to the power of the sun, wearing hats and long sleeved shirts while working outside in the summer. Everyone knew that the sun, like the use of tobacco, could cause cancer—Uncle Sam died of throat cancer, they said, "from smoking." There was a consciousness about smoking in those years even though few could or would resist the practice.

While the Hilltowners worked hard, including digging ditches in some cases, everyone had a dress suit for Sunday or Decoration Day. On this holiday, as well as Sundays and special days like funerals, men wore three-piece suits with fancy ties and shirts with French cuffs. Dark fabrics were favored, though on occasion in the summertime a light tan was fashionable. Shoes were dark and two tone, and when I think of the photographs Momma saved, I picture a guy in his three piece suit, ivy cap and a pipe in his mouth propping his foot on the bumper of a roadster.

Women had two looks; the older women tended to wear clothes from an earlier generation—plain dresses with long sleeves and skirts dragging the ground. Rarely did one see their shoes, much less a leg. Hats were also common to protect them from the sun, an awareness that seemed increasingly lost on later generations.

Younger women appeared different. My momma was an example with her knee length flowing skirts, tight waistlines and blousy tops with sleeves down to the elbow. I remember the high heeled shoes, as she and her sister Ina Mae were the only two I saw wearing them. At times Momma would seem to pose in those high heels, flowing dresses cut to fit her hourglass shape and shoulder length reddish brown hair framing a fair face with freckles and fashionable glasses.

But the thing that sticks so clearly in my memory is the automobiles—Fords, Chevrolets, and Buicks were the favorites but there was an occasional Cadillac or Packard. Some Sundays it seemed that we had a steady stream of the cars roaring past our house on that gravel and dirt Hilltown road. The dust flew as the grinning owners drove with windows and tops down. They were proud of their automobiles, which were a sign of success and independence they never felt during the six day work week.

Daddy and Momma each had their own automobile when they married in 1938, but soon compromised and sold Daddy's so they could furnish their new house—on Hilltown road, naturally. All this activity occurred at the end of the Great Depression and just before the war, but none of that seemed to restrain Momma and Daddy from with getting on with their dreams.

Strangely, Hilltown never really seemed to feel the brunt of the Great Depression. Oh, the residents of the little town were poor all right, but anyone who wanted a job had one. The Fries cotton mill was always hiring, and the railroad, the trucking businesses, the mines at Iron Ridge in Carroll County and the furniture factories of Galax all provided strong employment opportunities in those days. As the nation geared up for The War, all of these industries and other sectors operated at maximum capacity.

Looking back, I see those days as exciting. America prepared for war, fought it, won it, and transitioned to a new global economy. And my momma was an enthusiastic participant!

Although she did not finish the seventh grade and none of her brothers or sisters finished high school, Forest Gilley was determined that her children would go to college. It was understood from the beginning that we would go and that she would make a way. Actually, I seriously doubt that at the time of my birth she had ever seen a college—but knowing her, I can't say that with certainty.

My sister and I had more than 35 first cousins. Fewer than a half dozen ever attended college, and most of those were in a younger generation—Sister's generation. It is important to note that our father supported and echoed Momma's expectations, but not quite as loudly as she proclaimed them.

Momma spent a lot of time preparing me for school, and today her approach might be considered an early form of home schooling. Beginning and continuing with talking and reading, she soon introduced toys that I could take apart and put together. I later in life realized that everything Momma and I did was focused on learning. Without her family and others in Hilltown realizing it, she saw that I knew my ABCs and could read complete books two years before I was allowed to attend public school.

During those early years when I was two, three and four years old she would set aside time for reading. The things she wanted to read were not necessarily children's books, but books that she enjoyed. So fairly early she had me practicing my reading (even thought I didn't know I was practicing) by slowly going over specific passages from *Gone with the Wind* or the King James Version of the Bible.

Before we went to see the movie version of *Gone with the Wind* together, she read several passages from the book and selected passages for me to read. I had been going to the picture shows for some time but *Gone with the Wind* was so different with its color, and its characters seemed so real, unlike the cowboys and Indians shows. To me there was nothing quite like it until I saw *Giant* with Elizabeth Taylor and Rock Hudson.

However, my early childhood education went far beyond learning how to read, write and do arithmetic or going to the picture shows. We went places and saw things. Because Grandpa Windy worked for the Norfolk & Western Railroad, as did my father for a time, we could ride free on the train anywhere in the country—if we were willing to sleep in our seats. All we needed to do was ask Grandpa to get us a pass and we could have gone to California and back if we chose. Momma and I used free passes many times before I was five years old, beginning with riding to Galax and back on a Sunday afternoon, and evolving into longer and more adventurous trips.

For example, one Sunday morning in 1943 Momma woke me up and said, "Get dressed. We'll take the train to Nettie's today and have Sunday dinner." Nettie was Momma's oldest sibling. She lived on Chestnut Creek, not far from Galax with her husband Ruff and her three girls—Virginia, Mildred and baby Jessie, who was five years older than me. It wasn't hard to drive there, but the train ride was different and offered to be fun.

"Come on, come on," she said holding the car door open, and within minutes we were at the Fries Train Station, handing our passes to the ticket taker. The train was a coal fired steam engine, and clouds of smoke and some cinders were always flowing back into and around the passenger cars. I was afraid to stick my head out the open window, but did catch some red hot cinders with my hands. I thought there was no wonder Daddy used eye goggles when he was a train fireman.

But it did not take long for the swiftly chugging train to get down the River and up Chestnut Creek to a stop next to Rufe's farm. As we got off the train, Momma said, "We'll have to walk up to the house." It was about a half mile on a very dusty dirt road.

Once we got to Rufe and Nettie's house, I ran off with the other children to play. In due time the other kids ran off by themselves I was drawn to the barns and corrals and the animals. Cows, horses, hogs and chickens were everywhere.

However, it wasn't long before Momma called me in from playing with the animals and said, "Wade, it's time for you to come in and eat your dinner. All the grownups have eaten, and, besides, you are bothering Ruff's chickens running after them like that. He won't like that you know." That summons ended my day of playing, for after dinner I had a nap and then we walked back to the train tracks. After what seemed like a short train ride later, we were home and the whole Sunday was gone.

But not forgotten.

Momma and I made that trip from Roanoke to the Atlantic Ocean not once but twice—just the two of us, before I was five years old, which was very unusual for Blue Ridge folks. The remarkable thing is how well it all went. I was fascinated by the marvels of the ocean and the sea gulls, and I remember how she would tell our friends and family about our fun adventures. Going to the beach was not an 'in' thing in the early 1940s, with the war going on, and it certainly wasn't something the average person in Hilltown—or even urban Roanoke—experienced

After the long, six-hour train ride to the coast, we would take

Hoarce "G'burn" Hill in the mid 1920s showing the fashion of the day.

a trolley over to Ocean View beach. Once we got there Momma took me into the girl's dressing room and we changed into makeshift swimming suits. I just had some colored boxer shorts, while Momma had a blue striped contraption that looked like long underwear cut off at mid thigh and at the shoulders with an apron type thing around her waist. She was proud of her small waist—and of her more than ample hips and busts.... But we didn't have to worry much about our dress, for in those war years the beach at Ocean View was populated almost entirely by women and children. The men had other things to do.

We played in the water for hours. The beach was so different for a hill (billy) boy. The water was not like the river. It kept coming at me, lapping at and stroking at my ankles and legs. I just had the feeling that it was so much larger than life itself. The ocean was another world. These trips with a baby boy displayed an adventuresome spirit not present in many women of Momma's time.

From my point of view, Momma seemed more like Martha Jane and Martha Jane's mother, Elizabeth Kriegger than the original hill hugging Scots-Irish of the Blue Ridge Mountains. Martha Jane and Elizabeth were strong, independent women and who had minds of their own. Elizabeth survived her husband by twenty years, living into the 1890s and petitioning for and receiving delayed recognition as a Daughter of the American Revolution.

Whenever I think of Momma, I recall how she had provided more than just home schooling and broad life experiences for me. She was willing to sacrifice everything for her children's opportunities for learning. This lifelong commitment to learning and teaching of her children was the way my mother showed her love.

Momma never congratulated me on any accomplishments, even though I knew she was pleased. And at times I am sure she wondered about my wanderings, considering that her father had worked for the same railroad for 50 years and that his father had farmed his whole life. But she never questioned my judgment when it came to where I worked, just as she never asked to see my grades after I entered high school. (My college grades were mailed home addressed to my parents and they never once opened those VPI grade reports. There was a time while I was attempting to play college football that I was very glad they didn't.)

Momma felt that she didn't need to. She had already molded her son during his earliest years. It was more the direction than the exact path that she was concerned about. I now understand why she pushed me hard as a youngster, which was best expressed by her last words and the shaping memories of my earliest years.

Her last words said it all. She wanted one more opportunity to go over the game plan. "Wade, **we need to talk** like we did in Roanoke."

These are stories about *a time, a place, a boy and… A mother* whose ambitions for her children's opportunities through learning were without limits. Throughout her life she let her actions show her love but in the end she had no other choice but to reach out and tell me. Momma could not personally demonstrate by example so she chose to go back to the 1940s and tell me a lesson. And while she couldn't manage to conclude the conversation she did deliver her message to me. To Momma, that was all that mattered.

Home Alone with Momma

In my earliest years, Momma's presence was doubly important as America was in the midst of a terrible World War II. Although Hilltown, Virginia never saw a German or Japanese soldier, each of us was affected by the war one way or another, and Momma worked hard to keep life as normal as she was able during those years. Because of her, I was able to be a boy.

No Momma I'm not running Away!

"No Momma, I'm not leaving home, I'm not running away!" I yelled at the closed front door. It was a windy March day and I was wearing a coat. I struggled with the tiny, fully packed suitcase as I tried to convince Momma that I hadn't really meant to run away.

I had threatened to leave home, sure, but I didn't mean it. I was just kidding.

It all started early in the morning. We got up late and nothing seemed to go just right. Momma was busy because we had company coming and she expected Daddy to come in from Roanoke. She was anxious for him to get home as she wanted him to buy Uncle Sam's yearling so we could have our first milk cow. (Daddy would have his two-week paycheck from the railroad in his pocket and could make the down payment to Minnie.) Momma kept paced the floor before going to the sitting room window to look down Hilltown Road past Grandpa Windy's house. I caught her wiping tears from the corners of her eyes as she kept her vigil. Somebody else must have wanted that scrawny little red heifer, so she was worrying herself until Daddy got home.

I was bored with nothing to do and no one to play with. Several times I asked Momma if I could go and play with Ne-nee or Aubrey or some of the other boys. She always said, "No, Wade you can't 'cause you have a runny nose, the weather is too bad to play outside, and we're waitin' on your daddy."

Finally, after a midday snack of cold biscuits and sausage left over from breakfast, I was so cranky that she gave me a couple of whacks on the behind and sent me upstairs for a nap.

"Don't you come down 'til I say so," she said with her usual authority.

I wasn't sleepy. I roamed the two bedrooms and kept hollering down, "When can I come down? When, can I come down, Momma? Momma!"

Finally, I thought of another tactic. I came down the stairs and told Momma that I was leaving home. At first she ignored me completely and kept her watch out the sitting room window, dabbing her handkerchief to her red eyes looking for Daddy. She was more worried about that old heifer than she was me. Well, I was going to show her!

Suddenly she seemed to understand. She turned and looked straight at me ever so intently. "What did you say?"

"I'm runnin' away."

"So you're going to run away?" she asked. "Run away from home and never come back to see me or your Daddy? Is that what you're telling me?"

The very thought took me aback. "Well, no Momma I just said if you don't, uh... I'm going to run away from home."

"If I don't, you're going to...?

This was taking an unexpected turn. I needed to backtrack and get out of this situation, but it was too late.

"Well you come with me," she said. We'll see about this." With that she grabbed my hand and firmly led me upstairs to my room, started opening my chest of drawers and removing my clothes, neatly placing them into stacks and counting carefully as I watched. What was she planning to do?

I became very anxious as she reached under my bed and pulled out a small suitcase, the one I used when we went somewhere for an overnight trip—like to Roanoke or Winston Salem. With the suitcase spread wide open, she packed it full of my clothes and snapped it shut with a ring of authority that seemed to transform Momma from worrying about a heifer to taking charge and getting something done.

She turned, looking me up and down. "You'll need to be better dressed," she said as if talking to herself. I was all ears. Now what?

She went back to my chest and got out boxer shorts, a clean undershirt, socks, a clean dress shirt—my one and only. Then, she turned and went to the press and got my Sunday suit along with my Ivy Cap and from the bottom she lifted out my Sunday shoes. With all this she proceeded to fully dress me as though I was going somewhere special. She turned me and pulled me and had me put my arms through this and my legs through the pants as I began to protest. What in the world were we doing?

Within minutes I was fully dressed, with my suitcase in one hand and Momma holding the other, leading me straight down the stairs to our front door. There she opened it up and pushed me with my suitcase onto the porch. Pausing for a minute to look me over, and nodding her head as though approving of my appearance, she closed the door and left me outside protesting louder and louder that I did not want to run away.

Thinking back, there must have been a hint of a smile on her face, but that day I didn't see or hear any mercy.

I panicked. Down went the suitcase, off went the cap and now I was the one with tears flowing and my face red. I attacked the old six panel front door with both fists pounding it. "Momma, please let me in. Let me in. I didn't mean it. I'm not running away from home. I'll take a nap. I don't even want to play with Ne-nee." No answer. I whispered, "Please Momma."

The door slowly opened a crack. It was Momma!

She opened the door a little more and with a half smile said, "Wade do you want in? I thought you were leaving home?"

"No, Momma, I want in."

She opened the door wider, and bent to pull me into her arms as she swept me up and into the house, pressing me to her chest, patting me on my back and kissing my cheek. All of a sudden things were getting better. Everything was going to be all right.

In a few minutes we wandered to the side window and she lifted the curtain with one hand while she held me on her hip so that we both could see out as an image came into view from around the bend just below Grandpa Windy's house. We both caught our breath. Who was that? It was Daddy, he was home! Momma was delirious with happiness; she would get her heifer after all—unless Uncle Sam and A'nt Minnie had already sold it.

We ran to the porch and started calling to Daddy as he continued to walk up the dirt road. We were never happier.

Later that day, after Daddy finished off his sausage and biscuits, he went off and returned with a scrawny little cow. It looked awful, but according to Momma it was going to have a baby calf and we would have our own milk and butter.

We never discussed running away from home again. Momma had made her point.

Rushing to the Lewis Gayle

"Wade, come in here. And hurry!" Momma said. When I didn't reply immediately, she snapped, "Wade, I said come in here now and look in this jar."

As I slowly woke that cold March morning in 1943, I noticed Momma wasn't on her side of the bed. She was in the other room, saying something. I could barely hear her calling me to come. I just wasn't awake enough yet. Then she was standing over me dressed in her housecoat, with her hands on her hips insisting, "Wade I want you to come in here and look in the slop jar." When I didn't leap out of bed, she said "Now!"

Rubbing my eyes, for it was still dark outside, I said to myself, "Look at the slop jar?" Who would want to do that? Especially not a five year-old boy who'd been awakened from a deep sleep at six a.m. It was real cold, and the three quilts that Momma and I had slept under that night provided comfort and warmth that would be immediately lost as soon as I stepped out onto the freezing linoleum to go look in the slop jar.

Yuk.

In those World War II years, with Daddy gone most of the time, Momma and I slept together in her big warm bed. She'd moved us first to Pulaski and then to Roanoke for short periods of time, but we'd always come back to our roots in Hilltown. The Hilltown house was located next door to my Grandpa Alex (Windy) Hill's house and in those years it was as comforting to live beside my grandpa as Momma's three quilts were on a cold night.

These were the days before we had any indoor plumbing and so our toilet was an old fashioned outhouse. However, in the dead of a cold winter night no one wanted to go outside to use the outhouse, so most every house had a chamber pot, or slop jar, for use during the night. Now, it seemed that I was supposed to go look in ours.

As I wiped the sleep out of my eyes, I realized that something must be wrong. Momma had gone to use the chamber pot (slop jar) and came back very upset. She insisted that we both go look at the contents of the jar. When I looked down into the pot, I could see that the fluid was red, not yellow like usual. Momma said, "Wade do you see that? Did you do that?"

I shook my head, still too sleepy to care. "Wasn't me, was you."

Then she said, "You come here and use the jar while I look on."

That woke me up real quick. For me to use the jar while she looked was out of the question because I was a boy and she was a girl. No way. I had learned that you didn't do that. I hadn't done that in years.

But Momma insisted. With reservation and some irritation I pulled up my long night gown and began peeing into the jar. And there the pee came streaming out with a red tint. Momma was right after all, it was me, I was the one who had caused the slop jar to be red.

She took no pride in being correct; instead, she sounded panicky as she rushed down the stairs to call Pearl. Pearl Lambert was my daddy's sister and since and her husband, Doug, was away fighting the war, she was sure to be home. I could hear the two of them talking excitedly on the telephone. Then Momma hung up the phone and called Granny Hill who lived next door. Grandpa Windy worked for the Norfolk and Western Railroad and he, too, was gone much of the time. However the N & W had a way of taking care of its own. Granny would know what to do.

She told Momma, "Take him to the Lewis Gale." The Lewis Gale was the railroad's own hospital. It was located in Roanoke, Virginia, about eighty miles away as a crow would fly, but more than two hours of driving time over curvy two-lane roads. This hospital was the finest medical facility in all western Virginia due to the railroad employee union's backing and it was virtually free for railroad employees and their families. Like Grandpa, my daddy was now a train engineer and fully entitled to have his son seen at the hospital.

Momma phoned Pearl once again and told her what she had decided to do and asked her to come with us to Roanoke. She then proceeded to oversee my getting dressed, while at the same time throwing a few things into a small suitcase. We left the house in a hurry. Momma pulled on her wool jacket as we raced across the dirt path to our one car garage just as the sun was coming up.

We jumped into the dark 1930s sedan and I sat in the front as our car raced down Hilltown road on our way to Eagle Bottom to pick up Pearl. Momma talked continuously to herself as she drove the dirt and gravel road, through downtown Fries at rush hour (shift change for the cotton mill workers) and on down Stevens Creek Road to Eagle Bottom. Throughout Momma's life, she thought out loud and at times we did not know if she was talking to us or to herself. She definitely was not talking to me that morning. Rather, she was practicing what to say to Daddy, theorizing about how I had come to this condition and worrying about how fast she could get to Roanoke—all out loud as I listened standing in the back floorboard..

Under those particular circumstances it was not a comforting monologue .

She pulled to a stop in front of Pearl's house with tires skidding, rocks and dirt flying. Without a moment being lost, Pearl was down her front steps into our car. As Momma pulled out onto the road Pearl said, "How did it happen?"

Momma replied, "Don't know. He won't tell me what he was doing or anything that might have happened." Having by now been relegated to the back seat and there being no concept of anything like car seats or seat belts in 1943, I leaned across the seat and said, "I didn't do anything. I didn't!"

Momma promptly replied, "Wade, you don't know about this; I already know that. Now, be quiet, I need to talk to Pearl."

She then told the entire story of the early morning discovery and who she had talked to and what was said. Everybody thought that going to the Lewis Gale hospital was the right thing to do, or so Momma said. Pearl agreed and they made plans for logistics once they reached the hospital. It was clear Momma was planning to stay with me and Pearl was to handle the other details, whatever they were. Pearl might have to drive back home by herself as Momma would stay at the hospital if I stayed. I thought, *What did I do? Why is Momma so scared? She's never scared! I wondered if the fall off that cinder block pile might have done it but to tell Momma that would open a whole other line of questioning.*

I didn't want to stay in the Lewis Gayle but it was comforting to know Momma would be there right in the room.

The trip over the mountain roads through Ivanhoe, Fort Chiswell, Pulaski, Dublin, Radford, and Christiansburg and on to Roanoke was a wild one, for Momma drove without regard to any speed limits s if there were any back then. Reflecting back on that drive, I am surprised that we made it. In a six year-old Ford with no spare tires and no modern safety equipment zipping along at more than sixty to seventy miles per hour in the early morning traffic, we made the ninety-five mile journey in less than two hours.

I was checked into the hospital immediately as there was minimal red tape in those days. Once in the hospital room I undressed, got into a hospital gown and a nurse asked me for a sample in that pan she gave me. I looked around and there stood the nurse, Momma and even A'nt Pearl all looking expectantly at me.

The nurse recognized the look on my face and pulled a curtain around my bed with the authority only a nurse in command can exert. With just the two of us behind the curtain she turned her back and I filled the pan, once again under duress.

She opened the curtain, walked out with the pan in her hand and announced to Momma and Pearl, "Nothing here." What a surprise. However, Momma had brought the whole chamber pot to show anybody who needed to see it. The nurse took both containers for testing by the laboratory and for the doctors to see.

I settled into my bed while blood tests were taken and Momma was asked a series of questions. This was an overwhelming experience for a five year old who had been in a doctor's office only once before.

One thing was clear. I might be in a hospital, but I would still be sleeping in a room with my Momma. Within a couple of hours, a half bed was brought into our room and Momma unpacked her suitcase and placed her items in a drawer that slid out from underneath the bed. Arrangements were made for Pearl to spend the night with friends and we began to settle in shortly before dark. I had been seen by two different doctors. Each had several nurses and other assistants with him. They asked my Momma questions, and she in turn had lots of questions for them. They asked questions of me, too, but I could not tell them what had happened to me. I was too afraid.

Actually the only thing I could think of was a fall I'd taken the day before off a pile of cinderblocks Daddy had bought to rebuild the basement walls of our house. When I'd fallen, I had pulled several of the blocks down with me. I was so frightened of the tumbling blocks that I had climbed out quickly, dusted myself off and went on my way. I felt fine. In fact, I never felt bad at all during this whole ordeal, except when the doctors... well, did something very private and very unpleasant. That was an experience I could've done without.

The doctors said Momma was right to rush me to the Lewis Gayle, for I was bleeding internally. I'd lost half my blood and it might have been too late if she'd waited.

Momma and I stayed in the hospital several days, and I was

given three blood transfusions; one from Daddy and two from his coworkers at the railroad including a Mr. Dillon who was nice to me. The transfusions consisted of having the donor lie in a portable bed beside me while tubes were connected to both of us simultaneously. The procedure took about an hour or so, and during that hour, the donors always seemed to want to talk. Everyone wanted a confession as to what had really happened to cause such a loss of blood. But I remained mute on the subject, as I didn't want to get Momma upset.

During the nights as soon as the lights were turned down, Momma would get up and pull her bed over next to mine. Lying there, she would reach over and pat my arm just like I was a baby. But it was good to have her there and I knew she wasn't really mad at me.

After seven days I was discharged with a lecture from the doctor about the need to drink a half-gallon of water every day. Soon we were on our way back home to Hilltown. Momma returned to work in the cotton mill; I went back to Granny Gilley, who took care of me while Momma worked.

Life went back to normal, and there weren't any more medical emergencies, save the time Momma pulled the car door shut on my hand and broke my left index finger.

Eventually, I 'fessed up to what had happened on that pile of cinderblocks, and for several years Momma used the bruised kidney event as a point of reference when I needed some instruction or a cautionary lecture. She really never forgot because she probably felt that she'd been close to losing the boy she'd waited for for so long.

But at the time, all she said was, "Next time, just tell me."

The China Cabinet Falls.

"Oooh, Noooo all my china, all my china! I saved for years and it's all gone now!" Momma sobbed with her face in her hands. Her hair was soaking wet with kerosene and water and soap, and it hung down over her face and neck as she asked, "What will I tell Woodrow?"

Her older brother P'toke sat by her side patting her hand while attempting to comfort her. "It'll be alright Forest, it'll be alright. Woody will understand. He won't be mad."

I stayed huddled in the corner, wondering how the formal dining room had become such a mess so quickly. I had never seen Momma cry like that. It was scary to a five year-old boy.

My Momma was so proud of her dining room suite and the fine china she had saved for years to buy. From the beginning, she and later Daddy wanted a very traditionally furnished home with a formal living room, a formal dining room, an eat in kitchen plus the normal sitting room and two bedrooms. Their first house in Hilltown included six rooms with exactly that configuration. So from my first memories of living with Momma, we had a formal dining room with a mahogany table, six chairs and a matching buffet and china cabinet.

The China cabinet was Momma's pride and joy. Oh, the cabinet itself was very nice but what she was most proud of were the things inside. Momma had carefully accumulated a six place setting of China with all the matching serving pieces. She had several varieties of glasses. But her most interesting glasses were eight beautifully painted ones for iced tea. They had glass straws attached as a part of the glass, with a seashell-shaped lower end touching the bottom of the glass.

All of these were in the China cabinet when things went awry. Earlier that day, Momma had decided to paint the dining room. She'd been planning the project for months and had bought the paint and brushes and paint thinner weeks earlier. We had saved old *Roanoke Times* newspapers for days, and Momma had collected several chop sacks from friends and neighbors and washed them to use as rags for wiping up paint drippings.

When we got up that Saturday morning it was raining and as Daddy would be away working on the railroad that weekend, she decided that was the day to do the painting. Wouldn't Daddy be surprised when he got home?

So, shortly after breakfast we started collecting the materials in the dining room. First we moved the chairs with their varnished wood and padded seats into the living room. We spread newspapers everywhere, no paint was going to get on our lovely pine, tongue and grooved and varnished floor. Then we moved all the materials needed for painting into the dining room, placing them on a second layer of old newspapers.

My main job at first was to watch and talk to Momma, but as the day passed I graduated to picking up paint cloths, moving buckets, going for paint thinner and attempting to wash out brushes.

Painting the walls went very well, even though Momma was doing it with brushes. Paint rollers had not been invented or at least they were not used in Hilltown. She painted the baseboards and door frames the same color as the walls, leaving the six panel doors to be painted later. This part was finished by early afternoon.

Now she planned to paint the ceiling.

Momma used a step ladder with a little platform that held the paint bucket, paint stirrers and other necessary items including cloths to wipe up drippings. We moved around and around the room with Momma leaning over the table, now covered with old newspapers. Then the China cabinet got in the way. Momma promptly placed her bucket of paint on top of the cabinet and proceeded to finish up the job.

By now it was late afternoon. Dark clouds gathered outside and as the light began to fade, Momma began to hurry. To move things along she started having me help move the ladder. Then came the fateful event. I took some cloths from her while she stood on the ladder, brush in hand and the paint bucket on top of the beautiful China cabinet.

The step ladder started slipping.

I don't know if it was Momma leaning too much or what, but it started to fall. I looked up at her. She had this look of fright on her face as if for the first time in her life she was not in control.

She yelled, "Wade, Wade, grab the ladder!" I tried but the thing was too big and its momentum was too great for a five year-old to handle.

As if in slow motion, the ladder came falling down. Momma grabbed the China cabinet, and it fell with her, though thankfully not on her. The sound was deafening as the large piece of furniture hit the floor with a crash and its contents broke into thousands of pieces. And then the bucket half full of peach-colored paint sailed down, splashing as it fell. Momma's head and clothes were covered with paint. Her hair was full of it.

I was stunned for a moment, then screamed, "Momma, Momma, are you all right?"

She was okay physically, but her heart was broken and her hair was full of paint. She sat up, looked around and said, "Wade, help me up." Then she began to cry. Between sobs, she said, "Go outside and get the two gallon water bucket and the can of kerosene."

I ran and did as she said. We started cleaning up the mess, collecting the unbroken China and straightening the cabinet. Luckily, the floor had been protected by the layers of old newspapers. After a little while we were in pretty good shape and Momma began to clean herself up. She pulled her blouse off, poured kerosene into a dishpan and washed her hair with it to remove the paint. She shampooed her hair several times in soapy water in order to remove the kerosene.

But all this didn't cure her main woe—she had lost most of her beautiful dishes. Momma was heartbroken.

As we sat there in the dining room surveying the end result of our plan to simply paint the room, Momma was still sobbing quietly as our back door opened and in came her older brother P'Toke. He quickly assessed the situation and sat beside Momma, taking hold of her hand and quietly trying to calm her.

"I'll be alright, it'll be alright," he said.

It was, eventually, but Momma never forgot and never stopped regretting her losses. As was her way, though, she moved on to another day and other ambitions.

I never knew how she told Daddy of these happenings because that night as she tucked me in bed beside her the last thing I remember was her saying, "Wade, now I don't want you telling anybody about this. I'll tell your Daddy. You just keep quiet. This whole thing is between just the two of us. Okay? No use to get nobody excited."

Hurrying, I lose my Front Teeth

One warm spring day in 1944, I stood on our front porch high above the road and watched one man after another going into Daddy's garage, straight across from our house on the other side of Hilltown road. No one came out. They just kept going in; there must have been a half dozen by the time I decided to go over there and check things out. Why were they all going into our garage and not coming out?

    The old garage was where Daddy parked his car to get it out of the weather. It was a cinder block building divided into two parts. The section next to the road was our garage, and the section on the other side belonged to my uncle P'Toke Hill, Momma's older brother. Actually, the entire building had once belonged to P'toke and his wife, Callie, but when Daddy and Momma bought our house they wanted a garage, so they bought half the building for that purpose. The garage had two front doors, which met in the middle, but on this day one of those doors was open and the men were inside, avoiding the intermittent showers we were having.

    I peered in to the dark room and saw five or six men sitting on wooden stumps, upside down buckets or just squatting on the dirt and gravel floor. Someone said, "Come on in here, Awberry boy."

    I was a little cautious, even though by now I recognized them all as kinfolks. Several were smoking Camel or Lucky Strike cigarettes. Others were chewing tobacco and using their pocket knives for whittling on sticks, just passing the time with conversation or local gossip.

    Talking seemed to hush when I showed up but soon began again. They had been discussing whether or not the union was making any progress with efforts to organize the Washington Mills workers in Fries; and the fact that Aunt Minnie had just declared that Uncle Sam's throat cancer was caused from smoking. (No one questioned that conclusion but no one stopped smoking either.)

Then my cousin Leon Hill said he had just heard at the Jot'em Down store that Ethel had filed for divorce from her long time husband Fred "Baldy" Hill. (All the Hill's seemed to go bald around age twenty so why they called Fred "Baldy" I'll never know.) That really caused my ears to perk up. I didn't know much about unions or throat cancer; but I knew for sure that Momma would certainly be interested if Ethel was going to take out divorce papers. Cousin Fruitcake jumped in to tell about how Baldy had been brought home from Galax in the back of a pickup truck the past Saturday night. He was so drunk he had to be rolled out of the back of the truck into his and Ethel's front yard after having been gone for three days. He was unconscious and covered with mud from head to toe, and to make matters worse he didn't have one red penny on him. Instead of coming home as usual on Thursday night with his paycheck, he showed up drunk and broke on Saturday.

That was it for Ethel.

Baldy was my first cousin once removed, who'd worked on railroad construction for years, same as my Grandpa Windy. Their work took them to distant places, wherever the Norfolk and Western needed a bridge or a roadbed or whatever built. They worked in places like Bluefield, West Virginia or on the Narrows of the New River near the West Virginia border or in Glade Springs in the lower Valley of Virginia or in the coalfields of far southwestern Virginia and West Virginia. They would work ten hours a day for six days straight, rest on Sunday, and then work for four more ten-hour days before leaving the job mid-afternoon on Thursday to travel home for a long weekend. Baldy would have worked about a hundred hours in this two week period and drawn a big paycheck. He, like Grandpa Windy, was a member of the Brotherhood of Locomotive workers and received good pay and good benefits, including two weeks vacation each July.

While on the job, they slept in camp cars provided by the railroad at each construction site, and ate their meals there for minimum cost. These were prized jobs during the depression years.

Grandpa Windy worked for the N & W for fifty years before retiring around 1950 and was glad for the job.

However, there were drawbacks. The camps were lonely, and some men had difficulty coping. They needed more to do. Some were content after the work day to relax, smoking cigarettes and telling old and big stories (they were great story tellers.) Some liked to gamble. Some went looking for female companionship from time to time (It was rumored that my Momma had an unrecognized sister in a southwest Virginia town where Grandpa Windy had once worked for more than a year but I was afraid to check that out) and others took solace in alcohol. This boredom may have taken control of Baldy's life, or as some have suggested it might have been a genetic disposition. Whatever, he slowly but surely became a confirmed alcoholic. It was not his habit to drink every day, but on unpredictable occasions he would go on a binge and stay drunk for days.

Grandpa Windy and a couple of his other uncles tried to take Baldy under their personal supervision and sought treatment through the union's medical services, but he kept falling off the wagon. He was admitted to two different clinics for alcoholics, but still, every so often he would go on one of his binges and the life of his entire family would just fall apart.

He and Ethel had three children: Frank, or "Bib-boy," Alfred or "Firefly," and Betty Ann, or as they called her "Baby." Ethel worked in the cotton mill on second shift. They lived in a cute little house that Baldy's daddy had helped them acquire early in their marriage—as he had helped all three of his boys. Two of their children graduated from high school, Bib-boy went on to be an attorney after eight years in the army. Momma always credited Ethel with the successes of their children.

Ethel was from Floyd County and was a very religious person. She was a member of the Fries Pentecostal Holiness Church, which was located right there in Hilltown. She was a regular, being in attendance every time the doors opened unless she was working, or one of her kids happened to be sick. Though Ethel was mild mannered and had a wonderful personality, she did not cotton to drunkenness—especially from her husband.

From what was being said there in the cinderblock garage, the previous Monday she had gone to the court house in Hillsville, the Carroll county seat, and filed papers for divorce from Baldy. Divorce was not very common in those days; therefore, it was not made easy. Still, she had started the process. It became the talk of Hilltown for weeks.

As the weeks passed, Baldy sobered up and returned to work. He came home regularly, staying with one relative or the other. He was on his best behavior for the longest time anyone could remember. His paycheck came home and went straight to Ethel, who cashed it and issued just enough back to him to travel home at the end of his next work period.

During that summer, the Pentecostal Holiness church had their annual week long revival, which lasted late into the night. Baldy, to everyone's surprise, arranged to get off from work on the railroad, stayed with my Grandpa Windy and showed up each night at the Holiness church for the revival. Baldy had a gift of being able to talk anybody into anything– he was a natural born salesman and probably should have never been a railroad construction worker, but he was. The first two nights of the revival services, he attended by himself or with others including Momma's brother G'burn Hill and G'burn's wife Bertha Anderson Hill, herself a very religious person; but, soon Baldy was escorting Ethel to church. One night during the revival, Baldy was overcome by emotion. The Holy Spirit apparently reached down and touched him and he was saved. Before the summer was over, he was baptized in the New River at the old ferry crossing, downstream from Fries, and became a full fledged member of that church.

He and Ethel were back together, and their marriage was saved for a time. They eventually separated again and later divorced forever.

But back to that garage that fateful April day. As I stood in the garage, listening to Leon, G'burn and Foxy (all Hills) describe the story of Baldy being dumped from the back of a truck, I became overly excited. I just knew Momma would be anxious to know this. She couldn't possibly know, so I needed to get out of there to tell her this breathtaking news. Not wanting to disturb Leon's and the others story telling, I edged around the men, slowly exiting the garage through the door I'd come in. Then, I leapt over a ditch and ran across the road and headed for the gate to our front yard so that I could be the first one to tell Momma the news.

As I scampered up the five concrete steps to our front gate, my foot slipped on gravel and both feet flew out from under me. Down I went head first into one of the steps. The next thing I saw was red and began to feel the pain. I had hit my front teeth on the concrete step, and my mouth was bleeding like crazy. My ailing brought Momma hurrying to the front door. Seeing that I had fallen, she bounded to my side, picked me up, and carried me into the house as blood flew everywhere. Placing me on the sitting room couch, she rushed to the kitchen for a pan of water and towels.

I tried to tell Momma why I was hurrying home but she said, "Hush Wade, hush, we'll talk about that later." Soon I heard her talking on the phone to Daddy, who working in Roanoke that week. "Okay," she affirmed, "We'll take him to Dr. Blips in Ivanhoe as soon as you get home. His teeth look loose. Maybe...."

Maybe?

On Friday we pulled into the front yard of Dr. Blips' home/office and he took us straight in. We went to him because he kept evening and weekend hours. His office was in a side room attached to his white Cape Cod style home. He was the salaried doctor for the zinc company in Ivanhoe during regular daytime hours but saw others at night and on the weekends.

"So you fell, did you, young man?" The doctor said to me.

With his hand prying me mouth wide open, I could only murmur, "Uh huh."

He looked at Daddy and Momma and said, "You're right. They'll have to come out." And with that, he proceeded to pull a set of wire pliers out of his desk drawer and slowly but surely removed my six upper front teeth. Surprisingly, it didn't hurt.

That is how I lost my six baby teeth early, all at one time, causing the permanent ones to come in crooked, a problem Momma had me working on for years before she gave up. Every time I went to the dentist in the late 1940s and early 1950s, she would inquire about how to straighten my teeth. Each time, the dentist would give me a wooden paddle and tell me to spend my spare time prying one tooth against another. That approach never worked because, being in school, I didn't have any spare time to be prying my teeth apart.

But on the way home from seeing Dr. Blips that evening, Daddy turned and said over his shoulder, "Wade, why were you running up those steps?"

That's when I finally got to tell Momma, what I had heard earlier from the men in our garage, the news about Baldy and Ethel. I had forgotten until Daddy asked.

Momma, after letting me tell the whole story, looked at me and said, "Why, I already knew that, of course." She watched the trees flash past the moving car, then commented, "Wade, you should never hurry. See what it gets you?"

No Hangings Allowed Around Here

"Wade, Wade?" Momma said, as she walked from the upstairs bedrooms. "Where are you, Wade? You answer me, right this minute. You hear, boy?"

She was working on the second shift at the mill this week, and all morning had been frantically cleaning house and washing clothes. She only had a few minutes for me, and we had clashed a couple of times before she went upstairs to make the beds and bring the dirty laundry to be washed.

Now, coming down the stairs, her arms full of dirty laundry, she held her head sideways to see the steps, she continued to call, "Wade, Wade? Where are you?" Her voice grew louder as she approached the place where I'd staged my big surprise. "You had better not be outside on your own."

I'm here. I'm here. Look! I have a surprise for you! I thought. *I'm here. Hanging just like those guys in the 'The Hanging Time' we saw Saturday at the Picture Show. Look, don't you see me? Look over here. You can see me hanging off the staircase with my eyes rolled back and my tongue hanging out of my mouth.* I was standing precariously with a rope tied around my neck at one end and around the stair railing at the other. Both my feet were resting on two wood screws Daddy had left in the side of the staircase.

I really wanted to surprise Momma, and thought she'd be pleased to see me reenact the movie we'd seen together.

I heard her again but her voice was faint, "Wade come on out of there. We don't have time to play hide and seek today. I have to get ready to go to work. If I want to get to the mill by two thirty (she always wanted to be early, no matter what) we'll have to be over at Granny Gilley's in Eagle Bottom by two fifteen. We'll have to leave here in less than two hours and we haven't had any dinner nor made arrangements for your Daddy's supper. So, you come out of there and help me."

Come and help, I thought, still hanging there in the hallway. *I can barely stand here and I'm sweating. Come back. You'll be surprised.*

She didn't return. I heard her speaking to someone. "I see you, Shorty Hill, standing up there in the road acting like a big shot. I heard what you said, out there in front of the Jot'em Down last night." (Jot'em down was the credit system country stores used in those days.)

Momma continued talking to herself, "You are going to pay for what you said about Woodrow."

Seeing the object of her ire sitting down by the store had totally distracted her as she gave him a tongue lashing. She had forgotten about me, or so I thought.

"Wade," she said as I maintained my position hanging from the stair post. "If you hear anybody at the store say anything about your Daddy not paying his debts don't you say one word. You come straight home and tell me. I'll take care of it." She paused and I heard movement, then she continued, "I heard that Shorty last night. He is going to pay for that. He knows that your Daddy just changed jobs again and it will take a while to get on the payroll at the railroad. So what if we're a week late in paying our charge account at his store? That's no excuse to run folks down. Besides," she continued. "Shorty never held a full-time job in all his life for very long. Oh, he worked in the mill some, but that weren't for him. She snorted. "We bought this house just after you were born and borrowed over a thousand dollars. It's almost paid off. We can't pay our bills, he says. He couldn't even buy a house if his Pa hadn't helped." I didn't know whether she was talking to me, or Shorty, or to herself as she was wont to do.

Remembering me, she called, "Wade come out here to the back porch and help me put these things in the washing machine." I knew this was a ruse to get me out of my hiding place. She still didn't realize that I was almost hanging myself on the staircase.

She went on talking, or thinking out loud. "Pa gave all the boys some land and helped them with a house, but he didn't do anything for us girls. Not one thing! But when Ma wants something, who does she come to? Me, of course."

Years later this was proven to be very true. When Grandpa Windy died, Granny Flora Jane came to live with us. Then five of her offspring took Granny to court, attempting to force her to sell her one and only home. She knew that she would most likely never live there again, but she wanted to hang on to it. Paul Frost, the husband of Momma's sister Margaret, and Daddy hired a lawyer and got the suit thrown out of court. In the end, Windy's house sold at auction for some $2,200 after Granny died. It was enough to pay for her funeral plus each child getting $70 a piece for his or her inheritance.

Momma continued with a new tone of urgency, "Wade I'm running late. We've got to eat some dinner and finish this washing. Come out here and help me." I could hear her moving around. Why didn't she come on and find me, so I could surprise her before I fell and my surprise was ruined?

I heard the washing machine lid clamp shut and the motor start; chug, chug, chug. She had the clothes in and now she would find time for me.

But no! The water faucet came on and she was doing something at the kitchen sink. We were the only family in Hilltown with running water. Daddy made sure of that first thing after buying the house. Why he was so intent on this we never knew. He had never had it anywhere he had ever lived.

I was getting tired and had to readjust my foothold.

Momma was about fifteen feet away, with her back to me talking and running water into the sink. *What if this had been real?* I thought.

I could see her out of the corner of my eye as she let the water out of the sink, grabbed a hand towel and turning looked straight at me. She seemed to lean forward, peering at me while drying her hands.

"Wade? What are you doing? Why are you there like that?"

I was strung out standing there for so long and barely keeping my feet on the screws. The rope was getting tight on my neck. I said nothing.

Momma walked slowly toward me and then exploded. "Wade Gilley have you done gone and hung yourself? My baby. My baby. What have you done, now?" She yelled, rushing to my side, lifting me up and jerking the rope off my neck.

Momma carried me to the couch, laid me down and started blowing her breath into my mouth while shaking me. With all this going on I got short of breath and started breathing hard and began to open my eyes wider which Momma noticed and became even more excited. Seeing her in that state made me laugh. That was a mistake.

She sat upright and stared hard at me for a minute. Then she said, "Let me look at your neck." She yanked my shirt open. "No marks there!" she exclaimed, then got a certain look in her eye. *What is this?* I thought. *She knows. But what will she do? Kinda wish I hadn't gotten into this.*

Momma walked back into the room. She had a switch cut from the weeping willow tree Daddy had planted in the back yard next to the well house. It was not big but it wasn't one of those weepy things either. It was a serious switch.

She meant business. Now I was really wishing I hadn't gotten into this. Momma apparently didn't find my surprise as funny as I had.

"Wade, I'm sorry," she said, "I'm over it but you must have respect for your Momma. It seems the only way to get you attention is to get it."

"Uh oh," I thought to myself. "Am I going to get a switching? Don't she know I was just kidding?"

Easing into a sitting position on the couch sort of like a porcupine keeping everything in front of him I said, "I was just kidding Momma. Don't you know that?"

"Wade, this kidding went too far. This idea of hanging yourself is not kidding. I've noticed that you talk about hanging yourself from time to time and that worries me," she said, all the while stroking the weeping willow. "I've told you, your cousin Freefall and his daddy and his daddy's brother really hurt themselves, on purpose doing that,"

I'd heard of them finding "Freefall" Hill in the barn and that he didn't get his nickname until he was buried. But what did that have to do with me?

She continued, "You know one of my grandmothers had two brothers who supposedly died in the Civil War don't you? Well one of them was found in a barn, too."

Well, yes, I had heard stories about members of the Hill family getting so down that they hung themselves but what did that have to do with me? I wasn't no Hill. Besides I didn't even drink that moonshine like those Hills who got down so. (However, I was only five.)

"Ain't going to have no hangings around here, do your hear me?" she continued her pre-whipping lecture. "This is serious business."

Then she proceeded to give me a good switching all on the back of my legs where it hurt but did no real damage. It just made a point, I later decided. But it really did hurt and I cried and yelled.

She seemed exhausted when she stopped and was I glad. It had hurt like the dickens. "Just you remember," she said, "Ain't going to be no hangings around here. If anybody around here hangs himself, accidentally or not, he still gets a switching."

Time of Growing Up

In the life of every little boy there comes a time when he has to test his wings. That age came for me eventually, when it was time to push the limits a bit and try out what it would be like in the future, when I would be more than Forest's boy.

The Wholesale House

It was a warm early Friday evening in June 1944. Just as we did so many evenings during the World War II years, I sat with my mother, Forest Hill Gilley, in the sitting room of our house on Hilltown Road. This was before television, and radio reception was limited so nearly every night my momma and I would sit and talk—or read and discuss her books. From my very first memories she always talked to me as though I were an adult and we discussed anything and everything on her mind at any given moment.

Momma loved to listen to what we now refer to as country music with one of her favorites being Ernest Tubb's "Walking the Floor Over You." I was not as interested in that kind of music, or hardly any kind of music for that matter, but shared enough with her to have it etched in my memory. She also was an avid reader and insisted on me joining her in those worlds beyond our simple life on a dirt-and-gravel country road.

We were engrossed in a discussion of one of her favorite books that evening when my father came to the doorway and said in a low, serious tone, "Wade, I need to see you in the kitchen."

Momma whispered, "You better go on now."

I was startled.

My 31-year-old, 6 foot 5 inch, 230-pound father was rarely home during the war years of the early 1940s, and when he was home he almost never had anything serious to say to me. Daddy was an amiable man, almost always upbeat. In fact, there were only a half dozen times in the 56 years I knew Charles Woodrow Gilley that our conversations were anything but positive.

But his tone was not very upbeat that night. He was serious.

As we settled into our chairs across from each other at the small, white wooden kitchen table, I was apprehensive. Because it was the war years and Daddy was not at home that much, his visits were something to look forward to— but not tonight. It had fallen largely to Momma to make sure I was well behaved and knew the rules and expectations of our family. So to have a serious discussion with my daddy such as I instinctively knew to be coming was rare.

Daddy did not rush things and that made the tension even greater.

What was up? Had I done something wrong? All sorts of things ran through my mind as I sat there waiting for him to tell me what was going on.

Finally, Daddy said, "Wade, when you and Ne-nee went to the picture show last Saturday, where else did you go?"

Ne-nee was the nickname of my seven-year-old first cousin, Odie Funk. The previous Saturday, the two of us had been entrusted to go by ourselves to the movies in downtown Fries, about a mile and a half by a dirt road from our neighborhood of Hilltown. That is, we were allowed to go to the movies and come back without supervision, a relatively new thing for me but seemingly not new for Ol' Ne-nee, who was all of 18 months older than me and much, much wiser. Or maybe the term should be knowledgeable rather than wiser.

"Where did we go other than to the picture show?" I asked myself. It had been almost a week and a lot had happened that Saturday.

I remembered Ne-nee coming by our house to get me shortly

after eight in the morning and the clear instructions from Momma— stay with Ne-nee and be home no later than six in the evening because we would have dinner about that time and Daddy was home for the weekend. He worked as a railroad engineer for the Norfolk and Western Railroad and every other weekend he had three days off. This was the alternate weekend, which meant that he only had 24 hours off and he just spent Saturday night at home. Momma expected that we would have a family dinner together.

She gave me a quarter for the show, popcorn and a Coca-Cola. A dime bought all-day access to the movies, which included a cartoon, two newsreels and two feature movies—usually at least one western with Roy Rogers or Gene Autry and their well known sidekicks and horses. Frequently we boys would stay for two or three rounds of the same set of motion pictures—after all, it was 10 cents for two and one half hours or 10 cents for seven and one half hours.

Ten cents bought a bag of popcorn, only one size back then, and five cents was the price of a large cup of Coca-Cola.

All in all, she had been very careful in her description of her expectations for me with a lot of emphasis on staying with Ne-nee.

"Odie has been to the picture show lots of times," she said, "So you stay with him all the time. And, don't you boys get your bibs dirty." Bibs was her terminology for denim bibbed overalls, which most boys wore in those days. They had five pockets—two in front opening to the side below the waist, two in the rear just over the buttocks and one in the bib directly in front at chest level. The back pockets and the bib pocket all had buttons to secure the contents.

Odie's bibs seemed a bit tighter than mine and more worn with some recent patches. That was because his were older and mine were newer and looser. It was expected that two years was the life goal for such garments—if the owner did not wear or tear them out in a year.

Momma sent us off to the picture show; two boys with GI cuts (named for the haircuts soldiers got in those days) one with a full set of permanent teeth (Ne-nee) and the other with a partial set of permanent teeth coming in less than straight without the assistance of the six front baby teeth.

The rest was history about to be exposed.

In response to Daddy's question I gathered myself and said, "Well, on the way to the picture show we didn't take the road down to Fries." I paused to see if that was what he meant. "We went down the holler (a southern Appalachian term for hollow or small valley between steep hills), past Grandpa's spring house, past Doad Akers' house and on by the Sutphin brothers' place." I never knew 'Doad's' real name, but I could say that about a lot of people including some of my relatives.

Daddy seemed a bit surprised at this revelation. "Oh, you did, did you?"

"Yes," I said, being open to full discussion for indeed this was serious and I was, as usual, seeking Daddy's approval. "We stopped and looked at the old saloon near the Sutphin brothers' place." There were some unmarried Sutphin brothers who lived in their parents' old home place which included an old saloon built before the turn of the century and closed in 1919 with the passing of the 18th Amendment to the United States Constitution, prohibiting sale or consumption of alcoholic beverages.

Even though the 22nd Amendment repealed prohibition in 1933, the old saloon had never reopened and was a curiosity for everyone in the region. It was a clear piece of evidence that we had been a vibrant community even before Colonel Francis Fries, acting on behalf of the Washington Mills Company of North Carolina, had built the cotton mill at the Bartlett Falls on New River in Grayson County (assisted by and act of Congress) and founded and constructed the town of Fries between 1901 and 1903.

The Sutphin brothers were all in business of one type or the other —usually with the company— in or around Fries and they were not to be messed with—or so Ne-nee said.

I told Daddy, "Ne-nee wanted to go in the saloon but I wouldn't."

Ne-nee's offer had been attractive, since the old building looked just like a weathered version of the western saloon we saw in the movies in those days. (Anyone who remembers Festus striding out the swinging doors of the saloon in the classic television series "Gunsmoke" looking for Marshal Dillon can envision the look of the three-part faded orange-red building with "Saloon" on a big sign above the porch and entrance.) It was mysterious and we were naturally drawn to the old building.

But not that Saturday, as Ne-nee had responded, "Okay, let's go up to Top Street."

Daddy rose up off his seat and said, "Go up to Top Street?"

I could see this surprised him. My story had taken another and more dramatic, unexpected twist. Taking the short cut to Fries by going down the holler instead of using the road was one thing but then climbing the "mountain" to go up to Top Street was an entirely different thing.

"Where were you boys going, going up to Top Street?" he said as though he could not understand what in the world we were thinking.

"Well" I responded, "Ne-nee said there was an old water tank up there and we could throw rocks and see the water splash. We just left the path and climbed straight up the hillside through the bushes and trees all the way to Top Street." Actually, this was the town's old water supply tank. When the company built the mill and the town, including the 300 houses for workers, back in 1903 it had built a complete modern water supply system. It was the most advanced clean water system in all of Virginia at that time. In fact, Fries was on the cutting edge of sewage treatment, electrical power availability and telephone service throughout its first four decades.

That original water system included a small dam on a nearby creek, a filtering plant (the water flowed through a sand filter to purify it—more or less) and a pump station that lifted the water to the highest point in town, Top Street, where the natural pressure of gravity supplied the entire town with a steady flow of fresh water. Another system was built later, but the old reservoir was maintained for emergencies.

When we'd finally clawed our way to Top Street and stood up, there it was—the old water tank. It was a round concrete structure rising about six feet above ground with a conical roof. It was some 20 feet deep and about two thirds full of water. Around the sides were four windows, each about one foot by three feet.

Ne-nee ran over to the structure, slid down on his knees in the dirt and mud and literally put his head into one of the open windows.

He yelled, "Wade... Wade, come here look at the water."

I ran over to the tank, slid down on my hands and knees and looked in at the blue-green water with insects, leaves and other things floating on top. It seemed like a lot of water and something I had never seen before.

While surveying the truly amazing structure suddenly I heard, *Kapluk, Splash*! I was startled as the rocks Ne-nee was throwing down splashed into the water, sending ripples across the tank. It was exciting!

Noting my dumbfounded, amazed look, Ne-nee laughed. "Didn't know about this, did you? Boy, have you got a lot to learn."

I quickly joined in throwing rocks and clods of dirt into the water.

Ne-nee soon grew bored and so did I, to tell the truth, but he was the leader. We stood up and looked around. I was amazed. Looking out from the highest point in Fries I could see the big dam on the New River, the cotton mill itself and the maze of streets, paved streets no less, and houses and other buildings that made up the well planned town of Fries, Virginia. The ancient New River curved its way around the town and the associated suburb of Blair Town. The tracks of the Norfolk and Western Railroad, for which my Grandpa Hill worked for nearly 50 years, followed the river bank.

Then we spotted a brown 1938 Chevrolet winding up the set of streets leading up to where we were standing on Top Street. It was clear that this car was on a mission and it surely seemed to be coming toward us. I couldn't guess why and was gawking with intense fascination at the speeding car.

Ne-nee said excitedly, "It's Bruce Smith! Let's get out of here!"

With that he turned and scampered down the steep hillside we had climbed just a few minutes earlier. Not knowing who Bruce Smith was, I joined him and we ended up tumbling back down on the dirt road near the Sutphin brothers' place, dirty and breathing hard. Ne-nee sat there for the longest time, looking back up the hillside to see if we were being followed.

"Ol' Bruce Smith, he thinks he is so smart," Ne-nee declared. Now I didn't know who Bruce Smith was, but Daddy sure did and in due time I came to know him and his sister, Elizabeth, the Fries School librarian. Bruce was the chief and only policeman in Fries and, apparently, he was coming up to Top Street with a purpose that day. It couldn't have been what Ne-nee and I were doing but Ne-nee sure was anxious to get out of there and, as I said, he was a very smart boy.

With this revelation Daddy leaned forward as though stunned. "Did you see Bruce Smith? Did you talk to him?" He thought we were getting into trouble with the law.

"No, Daddy, we didn't," I replied. "We just went back down the hill to Sutphins' holler and we never saw him again all day."

He eased back in his chair. "What else did you boys do Saturday before going to the movies?"

I had to think a minute before answering. "Well, we got up and brushed the dirt off our pants and then went on down the road until we got to town."

"Did you go straight out Church Street to the picture show?" Daddy asked.

The fact was that once we got into town, we should have turned right on Church Street, and within a few hundred feet we would have been at our intended and authorized destination, the Fries YMCA building and the picture show.

"Well no," I admitted, "we went on over past the school house to Railroad Street (now Riverview Drive) and then we went downtown."

That is, we had avoided going directly to the show because Ne-nee said we had time to go downtown and there was something he wanted to show me.

"So you boys went downtown instead of going to the picture show? Exactly, where downtown did you go?" Daddy insisted. It seemed he was getting to the bottom of his inquiry. It was about over, that inquisition. We all could go on to bed.

But his question was not that simple to answer.

With all that went on that Saturday I needed to focus on what we had done downtown. I took a moment to think about it before replying, "Ne-nee said we needed to go to the hardware store, so we did."

"The hardware store?" Obviously Daddy was surprised again as my story took another unexpected twist.

"Yes, we went to the Company Store. We stopped in the drugstore first, looked through the grocery store and the men's clothing store before ending up in the hardware store," I quickly stumbled through several of the stops we had made on our way to the hardware store.

Actually the hardware store and the other stores were all part of the Company Store, built by the Washington Mills Company back when the dam, the cotton mill and the town were all built between 1901 and 1903.

The Company Store stretched out on the south side of Main Street, which led to the mill itself. Also included in the Company Store were a barber shop, a beauty shop, the doctor's office, the U. S. Post Office, the Masonic Lodge (Dixie Lodge #202, I later learned when Daddy and I were members), a dentist's office, the town hall, a women's clothing store and, of course, in the basement of this long, three-story structure a well developed hardware and home fixtures store.

The Company Store was basically characterized by its comprehensiveness—something of a Wal-Mart of yesteryear—and its community pervasiveness. To quote country singer Tennessee Ernie Ford, everyone "owed their soul to the company store." Those who worked for the cotton mill could charge almost anything they might need and have it deducted from their paychecks. The problem was that before long, individual workers and their families owed everything to the company store including, if one believed Tennessee Ernie, "their souls."

The hardware store was a special place for two country boys. It had everything—nails and screws, hammers and saws, large pieces of equipment, cook stoves, Warm Morning heating stoves and, of course, Frigidaires, even though a lot of folks in Fries still used ice boxes for cooling their food and had blocks of ice delivered to their homes twice each week.

Even though it was Saturday morning and business was brisk, Mr. Bud Jennings, the hardware store manager, had noticed two very young boys wandering alone—and nearly overwhelmed by the sights around them—through his domain.

Ne-nee darted from one object to another, occasionally bumping into real customers and distracting Bud Jennings' attention from business.

Soon, while we were totally absorbed looking at fishing equipment, Jennings came up from behind and grabbed us by our shirt collars, practically lifting us off the floor, and ushered us out the door into the back alley and onto the railroad tracks behind the store.

"It's time for you boys to be on your way. Git, git, git," he ordered as he roughly tossed us out from what seemed to be Nenee's favorite place in all the world.

It was not the story Daddy was looking for. "Did he call Bruce Smith or anybody?"

"No," I said, "He just shoved us out the door. He didn't want us in the hardware store."

"What did you boys do then?"

"Well," I said, "this man named Booger Mullin (didn't know his given name) came out of the store and stopped and started talking to us."

"What did he say?"

"He said, 'did we like to fish?'"

"Like to fish? Why did he say that?'"

"Well, Mr. Mullin had this fishing pole and he had been in the hardware store looking at all the hooks, lines and sinkers they had there. He said he was going fishing and wanted to know, would we like to go with him."

Daddy paused for a moment or an eternity, depending on where you were sitting. "Did you boys go fishing with that Mr. Mullin?"

"Well, yes... uh, uh... no. I mean we followed him to the river where he was going fishing, but we didn't fish 'cause we didn't have any fishing stuff like poles and such."

"Tell me exactly what you did do," Daddy said in a tone I knew all too well. Now he really meant business.

I told him how we followed Mr. Mullin up the railroad tracks toward the Fries Dam and past the end of the Fries floodwall, built after the 1937 floods along the Ohio River and its tributaries, including New River. Downtown Fries had been flooded as were other towns and cities involved in that great act of nature. Shortly thereafter the federal government had built most cities and towns impacted by the flood concrete flood walls designed to hold rising waters away from their business districts.

We continued to follow Mr. Booger, a unique Fries character as I later learned, almost to the looming brick cotton mill itself before we turned toward the water and continued along the river's grassy edge toward the dam.

Booger spent much of his time fishing because few people would or had the time to associate with him. He had a 4-F draft classification, meaning he was unable to serve in the armed forces by reason of either physical or mental impairment.

My thoughts were drifting when Daddy interrupted me sharply and said, "How close did you boys go to the dam?"

"Well," I reluctantly admitted, "real close."

The Fries Dam had been built in 1901 by Colonel F. H. Fries, a well known North Carolinian from the Winston Salem area, to harness the natural power of the New River at Bartlett Falls and generate enough electricity to power a huge cotton mill plus enough excess electricity for a town of 300 homes and much of the nearby countryside. (Among other accomplishments, Colonel Fries oversaw the building of a 112-mile railroad from Winston Salem to Roanoke, Virginia and founded the Wachovia Bank in Winston Salem, for which he served as president until he was 75 years old.)

Fries Dam stretched more than the length of a football field from the virtually vertical southern hillside over to the more gently sloped northern side of the New River—Bartlett Falls it was called in the federal law authorizing the dam in 1901. It was about 35 feet high and a great abundance of turbulent water flowed over it, hitting the riverbed below with a continuous thunder. Ne-nee and I could not hear each other speak as we approached the dam's base.

The water had dredged deep pools at the base of the dam and that was where Booger was going to fish for carp and other bottom-dwellers. The larger fish were attracted to both the deep water and the various species of life the river pumped over the dam and into the pools. It was a great place to fish.

Booger turned as he approached the base of the dam and waved his hand in a way as to say, "Come on, boys, this is where the fish are. I'll let you use my rod." Even though we could not understand a word he said because of the thundering roar of the falling water, we knew what he meant. We were to be part of this adventure.

Ne-nee and I hustled on to catch up. Booger turned and started skipping from rock to rock to get out into the middle of the river and close to the larger pools of water, right under the middle of the dam. We followed but instead of skipping from rock to rock we ended up jumping from one to another.

"Ne-nee fell off one of the slick rocks and went in over his head," I told Daddy, "but he popped up and grabbed the rock and climbed out."

Daddy became red faced and agitated. "Wade, did you fall in too?"

"Well, no but I slipped and got my shoes all wet."

"Did Booger Mullin talk you boys into going out there?

"No," I answered, "he asked and Nenee really wanted to do it. So we went out there with him. It was really fun. We just stood there and watched the water coming down; it was higher than the Company Store. That water really made a noise when it hit the rocks and splashed everywhere. And Mr. Mullin caught this big fish. A carp, he said. It was so big he had to take it over to the river bank to kill it with a rock before he went back to fish for more."

"How long did you boys stay there in the water at the dam?"

"Oh," I said, "we left after Mr. Mullin killed the carp. Ne-nee said we needed to go because it was time for the first picture show to start."

"And, you went straight to the picture show?"

"Yes, we went up to the YMCA and around to the Church Street side and went in. We were a little late as everyone else was already in their seats." (Not quite but close.)

The Fries Theater was part of a larger structure that included a YMCA with pool tables, a bowling alley, a snack bar with delicious hotdogs and a gymnasium (the first in western Virginia) along with a library and meeting rooms for the Lions Club and other civic organizations. The theater itself was divided into three viewing areas. You went in the front door and straight to the ticket booth. After buying your ticket you could go in a door to the right just by the restrooms or a door to the left which went by the concession stand where the Cokes, hotdogs, popcorn and candy bars were sold.

To the far right, above the restrooms, was a set of stairs that led to the projection booth and about 20 seats in a balcony box for important people, including the company bosses and their families. They did not socialize with the regular folks except to use the bathrooms—if they did.

To the far left, beside and over the concession stand was another set of stairs leading to a second box of about 20 balcony seats. This was for the town's few black residents, or as they were referred to in those days, Negroes or colored folks.

Everyone else had to sit in the 150-seat main theater, on occasions looking back over our shoulders at those balconies and wondering what it would be like to sit there. The irony of these two groups of special people, company bosses and Negroes, sharing prime balcony seats divided only by a wooden railing, was lost on me at the time. Today I wonder if that thought ever occurred to either group.

One thing I still do not understand is where the blacks went to the bathroom. One never saw any of the bosses in the men's room either so there must have been some special arrangement that I never knew about.

Fries, like the rest of the South, was legally segregated but the bite of discrimination seemingly was not as harsh as it was in other parts of the South. I remember my father doing business with African Americans just as with anyone else. He always bought his piglets from a black farmer up in Grayson County. We slopped those pigs with chop—a ground mixture of wheat, corn and molasses mixed with water. We slaughtered the grown and fattened hogs in the colder November weather.

The western mountains of Virginia were sharply divided in Civil War days and for decades afterward. Many had been in sympathy with the Northern forces, accounting for the strong Republican leanings in the Fries area. There were two clans with one extended Hill family (my mother's) being partisan Republican and the other avid Democrats. The split originated when two Hill brothers chose different sides in the 1860s.

After I told Daddy that we went straight to the picture show he looked at me for what seemed a long time and asked, "You didn't go anywhere else?"

"No. After Mr. Mullin killed the carp we ran all the way to the show."

What could he be looking for? I had told him everything we had done that day and still he was pushing me for more. Daddy leaned back in his chair. "Wade, what about the Wholesale House?"

"Oh, the Wholesale."

The Wholesale House was huge warehouse, associated with Washington Mills of course, for the distribution of dry goods, canned foodstuffs and other things to the country stores around the Fries area. Items could be bought in bulk there—hundred pound sacks of chop, cases of Carnation evaporated milk, boxes of candy and peanut butter crackers—Nabs—and many, many other things. The building was just east of the Company Store, right on the railroad tracks and next to the White Flash gas station and Hester's Dry Cleaning.

One side of the red metal-sided, two-story building with a gabled roof opened to the street where trucks were loaded and customers entered while the other side had a large door opening to the railroad tracks where incoming cargo was unloaded from the freight cars. This was before the days of interstate highways and rail was the overwhelming means of longer distance transportation of goods of all types. At either end of the building were large doors on tracks to be slid open and shut where trucks backed up to load or unload.

I can remember going to the Wholesale many times with my father to buy animal food in bulk or 50-pound bags of cement. Daddy was a carpenter and brick mason on the side, and he purchased his raw materials there.

Needless to say this was a very busy place on a summer Saturday in the booming economy of the region as the war was being won. It was full of people.

The Wholesale was one of the many attractions Ne-nee introduced me to that day. "Let's go in here!" he'd said, "They have everything!"

As I told Daddy the rest of the story I sensed that this was what he was after all the time. He was undoubtedly surprised by all the other confessions he had drawn out of me.

"Daddy, we just went through the Wholesale and nobody even noticed us. We didn't stop or get anything."

"Oh, yes," he said. "Uncle Horace was there getting some supplies for his store and he saw you boys in there and told me you were going to get into trouble if we didn't watch out. Little boys do not have any business being in the Wholesale without their parents," Daddy said, "and I don't want to hear about you doing that again. Do you understand me?"

He didn't have to shout for I heard him clearly the first time and I really did understand his point. Still, I was relieved because I thought that we must have done something really bad when Daddy started his questioning more than an hour before. Ne-nee and I had just been in the wrong place—several times.

About that time Momma came to the kitchen door. "You boys have been in here talking a long time. Don't you think it's about bedtime?" It was after eight o'clock and past my bedtime. I was ready to go.

But Daddy said, "Well, I think we all ought to talk some more. Forest, could you come in here and set a bit with us? You need to hear Wade's story about last Saturday when he and Ne-nee went to the picture show."

That led to a full recounting of Saturday's experiences for Momma, an expedited one with a lot of prompting from Daddy.

The second telling was easier for me and, I think, for Daddy but I'll never forget the look on my mother's face. When her baby had left for the movies that Saturday and returned within the prescribed time, she little dreamed that he had seen so much adventure.

As the telling went on she frequently put her hand to her mouth and declared, "Oh!" or "Oh, my!" and "My, my!"

While Daddy made a series of unforgettable points before I went to bed that night, Momma never, never (almost) let me forget it. For years it seemed when she would let me go somewhere with someone else she seemed compelled to bring up the Wholesale House story in one way or the other.

As we left the kitchen to go upstairs to my bed, Daddy paused. "Wade, wait just a minute. After you boys went to the movies Saturday where else did you go?" Obviously, it had occurred to him that there might be still more to our adventuresome day.

But that did not work

Momma turned, adjusted her glasses and stood to her full five foot seven inches—remember she was the second tallest person in all Hilltown—and declared, "Woodrow that will have to wait. We are going to bed now."

And so we did. That is, after she read me another story and did some subtle questioning of her own that elicited even more information.

After all, who could lie to Momma? Who would dare to?

Queenie, My Queenie

One day, while I was standing in front of Alvin Caudill's Jot'em Down store on Hilltown Road, cousin Roy Hill walked up with his 22-caliber bolt action rifle loosely thrown over his shoulder and said to me, "Wade, where's your Daddy?"

"He's inside," I replied.

"Did y'all bring ol' Queenie with you tonight?"

The question, the rifle and Roy's very presence created a sense of uneasiness in me. Was this the time? Was Roy going to be the one to put Queenie down?

"Can't it wait?" I asked, knowing in my heart and stomach that he was there to take Queenie into the woods and shoot her. She was sick and Daddy didn't have the stomach to see her in so much pain. So it had to be done. But Daddy couldn't do it and I certainly couldn't. Roy could and would, for he owed Daddy some favors.

"Up to your Daddy," Roy replied, "he just asked me to do it."

"He's inside," I said, and I started easing down the road toward home just wanting to get out of there but waiting to see what Roy did.

Roy went inside and in a few minutes he came out and I heard him whistle for Queenie. She came to him so friendly wagging here tail and together they took a path into the woods. It was the last time I would ever see my companion, the dog I loved like a brother or sister or even like a Daddy. I am sure my Daddy felt the same way if not more so. She meant so much to him and he felt he was the cause of her suffering.

We got Queenie in about 1943 when Daddy satisfied his itch for bird hunting by trading his new seventeen jeweled Elgin wrist watch for a ten month old pure bred English Pointer and a sixteen gauge pump shotgun. The watch had cost Momma about a hundred dollars when she bought it for Daddy the year before—the equivalent of about a month's wages for the both of them. He was proud of the watch, and so was she, but he traded it for a gun and a dog. While she hadn't made a public fuss over the trade, it was a bone of contention for years.

There were two types of bird dogs in Southwest Virginia in those days—English Pointers and English Setters. Setters were long haired and resembled Collies or Shepherds. But the short haired Pointers were favored because of the rough terrain, and because their white and brown coloring made them more visible in the brush.

Queenie was a purebred Pointer. She was easy to train and quickly became the talk of the whole area in discussions of bird hunting. Many times other hunters attempted to borrow or rent Queenie, but there was no way Daddy would allow it. She was his pride and joy.

She became my constant companion in those days, as both of us were kept inside the white picket fence that Daddy had built around our yard. At times, we both patrolled the front fence talking to anyone who passed by with Queenie just being friendly, and me hoping to attract someone to come in to talk or play. She was a protector as well and would not tolerate adults coming too close to me or the house without the approval of Momma or Daddy.

When she was three or so, Queenie gave birth to a litter of purebred pointer pups and became the talk of not only our Hilltown people, but of the whole area. Bird hunters from Galax, Wytheville and Pulaski came to see for themselves the two pups that survived. They were interested in their appearance—their coloring, markings, etc.—as well as how they were advancing in their specialized training. When they were about four weeks old, each pup (named John and Samuel) could point anything and everything on command, and by the time they were a year old Daddy had recouped his original investment as lots of people waited in line to purchase the dogs. He sold them for a good profit but never seemed to have the money to get another seventeen jeweled Elgin.

When I was about ten years old, Daddy brought me into the hunting equation. He bought me a bolt-action, single shot 22-gage rifle and invited me to various hunting events, which were usually held somewhere on the back part of the original Hill property between Hilltown Road and the New River. This acreage had corn fields, overgrown pasture fields and other good places to hunt quail and mountain grouse. However, to hunt ring-necked pheasants required traveling as far as Iowa or South Dakota. I did not get invited on those trips.

A hunt for birds began with taking Queenie to one of the fields and in spread file fashion march behind her as she systematically covered the assigned territory with her nose to the ground sniffing for birds. She was never distracted by animals such as rabbits, squirrels or coons. It was difficult to encourage her interest in birds other than the game birds for which she was trained to hunt. Therefore, she ignored robins, crows and the like.

When Queenie smelled a game bird such as quail or mountain grouse, her whole demeanor changed. Her actions became very systematic, even businesslike, as her walk became a half-crouch position with her nose pointing in the direction of the game. A certain tenseness came over her, illustrated by her tail, which stood upright and straight as an arrow. When she identified the game being hunted either through her sharp vision or keen sense of smell, she became even more cautious and focused. This rigid stance— nose and eyes focused on the game, body tense with tail upright and straight while lifting her right foot—created a model of an arrow directed at the target. When the birds saw her thus, they became transfixed or prematurely traumatized. They could not move as Queenie pointed them out for the hunters to see

The hunters approached their dogs cautiously from the rear so as to locate the birds. Usually the birds could be viewed in a hunkered position close to the ground, slowly easing away in the opposite direction. Once we hunters were in position Daddy would say, "Go git 'em girl! Git 'em!" Then Queenie would leap into the flock and flush them into flight. At that time, the sporting thing for hunters to do was shoot at the birds while they were in flight attempting to escape. Daddy was an excellent shot and usually could take two or three birds with his sixteen-gauge, pump-action shotgun.

As the shooting began, Queenie would first ensure that all the birds were in the air, and then on Daddy's command she would search out and find the downed birds. On finding a shot bird—wounded or dead—she would first carefully crunch it in her jaws such that their bodies were not damaged, but they could not escape. Next, she would deliver the bird to Daddy and trot off to retrieve the others. She could remember as many as five birds falling, locate each individually and one by one deliver them to Daddy without further instruction.

At the end of a hunt Daddy brought his catch home and together we dressed the birds, keeping only the breasts of either quail or grouse. Four to six baked or roasted quail breasts made a very nice platter when Momma surrounded then with cooked potatoes, onions and carrots complemented with biscuits or cornbread.

When I hunted birds as a twelve year-old boy, the routine was different. By then I had my own shotgun, but for me to hit a flying bird was highly unlikely. This created a need for Daddy to provide me with a little advantage. He did this by allowing me to shoot at a bird while the flock was still on the ground. My shot became Queenie's signal to flush the birds. Once or twice I killed a bird on the ground, but Ne-nee proclaimed this act of shooting a bird not in flight to be illegal when he heard me brag of my success.

Frequently, Daddy took Queenie across the state of Virginia and occasionally even to the Midwest to hunt birds and show her off. I never experienced these trips while she was alive.

Some months after Queenie delivered her first litter of puppies she came into heat again. Momma noticed it and called Daddy, who was at work out of town. He instructed Momma to lock Queenie in the secure pig pen. That tactic had worked time and again 'cause Daddy didn't want Queenie to be just a producer of pups. But this time something happened that changed everything.

By the time Daddy came home she seemed fine and he turned her loose to roam our property as before. Within few weeks, however, Daddy noticed that Queenie was getting larger. To everyone's surprise, she was going to have another litter of pups. The real concern came when she gave birth to six puppies while Daddy was away at work. The newborn pups were about a week old when Daddy returned home. He immediately saw that they were not purebred bird dogs, which was something he had feared all along. He concluded that they were part Red Bone hound dog and that Grandpa Windy or someone had let a Red Bone in the pen while Queenie was in heat. For years Momma would cry when we talked about Queenie and say *why did Pa do that?* 'cause after all, Windy was the only person in Hilltown with a Red Bone.

The Hills were like that. Purebred meant nothing to them, and besides, they were not especially fond of birddogs.

Daddy was upset at this turn of events because of the delicate nature of cross breeding. He was right because the next week while he was away working the pups got sick one after the other and died. The problem was that now was too late as Queenie was fully prepared to nurse the six baby dogs—her breasts were full. Had the babies been taken away from her the first day after birth, she would not have developed full nursing capacity and could have quickly adjusted.

However, after the pups' deaths her full breasts became swollen, red and painful for her. This condition did not subside in fact it continued on for months, until one day Daddy loaded Queenie in our car and was off to Rural Retreat to see the veterinarian—the only one in our part of the State. Rural Retreat was located in Wythe County more than twenty miles away over curvy country roads.

One look and the veterinarian stepped back, looked at Daddy and proclaimed, "She's got breast cancer."

I left the operating room. During the next two hours, the vet conducted major surgery on our Queenie. Afterwards, he sewed her up and gave Daddy precise instructions for removing the stitches and treating the wounds. We headed home, a sad, sad lot. Queenie was moaning and groaning, I was crying and Daddy was petting her, all the while chastising himself for what had most probably caused this crisis in our lives. If he had been more careful in shutting her up, this never would've happened.

As the weeks went on, Queenie seemed to recover and she even hunted again that fall. But eventually the cancer came back and she ended her life a mere shadow of her previous self. We lost our champion bird dog and our loved companion.

In due time, it became apparent that her days were numbered and that her suffering was unbearable. It was clear that her hunting days were over and where she was headed.

This was the first time I had heard the concept, "Put her out of her agony, that's the best thing to do. Spare her the pain." These words came from Daddy. He felt the pain as much as I did.

"Come on Queenie," I heard Roy say as he came out of Caudill's store. "Come on let's you and me go over in the woods. You'll like those woods 'cause they have lots of birds."

As they entered the woods, I turned and ran home to my room. There on the bed I mourned my dog and didn't come out of my room for hours. Not until Momma called Sister and me to supper. We all ate in a silence that was deafening on that evening. The mourning was felt by everyone, even my three year-old sister who barely understood that Queenie was gone. Momma still cried when she talked about Queenie more than twenty years later.

I suppose none of us ever really knew the pain Daddy felt.

Only once over the years can I recall a discussion of Queenie's end. Oh, we talked about all the fun times we had with her; and, to hear Daddy tell it she was the smartest, friendliest, prettiest and best Pointer dog that ever lived. I believed that, too. And I still do. Queenie is long gone, but I still have my memories of the smartest, fastest, bestest bird dog in Hilltown.

And I still have that sixteen gauge shot gun that Daddy got when he traded for Queenie in '43. He never had another pure-bred Pointer or a seventeen jeweled Elgin watch and he never forgot Queenie. None of us did.

Going 'Coon Huntin'

Just before dusk on a brisk November afternoon our telephone rang—two shorts and one long—we were still part of the party line system in Hilltown.

"Hello," Momma said. After listening for a minute she said, "He's here, but Woodrow won't be home until after nine o'clock."

She listened for another moment, and then exclaimed "What? Coon hunting? Well, we'll see—let me call you back."

She hung up the phone and turned to me. "Wade that was Grandpa. He wants to know if you would like to go 'coon hunting tonight."

Go coon hunting? I had heard talk about coon hunting ever since I could remember and had always wanted to go. The Hills took their hound dogs, stayed out all night and brought home raccoons to be skinned for their fur. I had seen coonskins nailed to many smoke houses and tool sheds. This was something I really wanted to do. It meant that I was no longer considered a child but ready to move into another circle.

Without any hesitation I nodded, "Yes Momma. Yes, I want to go. Can I? Can I go?"

She seemed both amused and a little troubled. "Well," she said, "your daddy isn't here and I don't know if I should let you go without him knowing about it."

"Please Momma, please," I begged. Going 'coon hunting with the Hills was a family ritual. There had been coon hunting in Hilltown ever since John Robert Hill, my great grandfather, was a boy in the 1830s and maybe before. I had never been invited in the past—it was a coming of age in the Hill family.

At last, she relented to my pleading and called Grandpa back to say she was dressing me warm and that I would be over to his house shortly. She then turned to me and repeated everything she had just said to her daddy, adding, "He said you would be back before midnight and you had better mind. Do you understand?"

"Yes Momma, I understand, and I'll be sure to mind Grandpa Windy."

Oh, boy, I though to myself. *This will be great!* I was finally going to go coon hunting. We would be taking several coon dogs and rifles. And we would stay up until midnight!

Then Momma dressed me. I needed a warm coat (my mackinaw would do fine), a toboggan that could be pulled down over my ears and extra thick socks (or two pair) inside my high-topped brogans, which came up over my pant legs and tied around the calves of my legs. This would allow me to tramp across the fields and through the briars and woods so I could follow the coon dogs without getting my legs full of thorns.

When I got to Windy's just at dark he was ready and so was my eleven year-old cousin Ne-nee, who lived with Grandpa Windy and Granny Flora Jane. Windy's 'coon dog was tied to the fence just outside the kitchen door, ready and waiting. In addition to the rifle, kerosene lamp and flashlight, Granny Hill had packed us a big lumpy canvas bag.

I wondered, *What is in that bag? Maybe Grandpa Windy will let me carry it.*

When everything was ready, Grandpa Windy said, "Grab this stuff and let's go, boys." I quickly grabbed one of the canvas bags and we left through the kitchen door, and took our dog by its leash. We crossed the apple orchard south of Grandpa's small farm and headed toward Uncle Sam's farm. Ne-nee and I followed close, carrying what we could. We were on our way to a rendezvous point about a half mile west of A'nt Huldy's house on a knoll overlooking the great bend of the New River in one direction and the Double Shoals the other.

When we arrived, I was surprised to see that Grandpa Windy's brothers Possum and Ellis Hill plus several nephews including Roy Hill and Dollar Bill were already there. I was glad to see two other boys in addition to Ne-nee and me—She'dan's boy Willie, and Dirty Hill—whose nickname need not be explained.

This was going to be a fun night. My first coon hunt.

The others had a fire started inside a three-foot circle surrounded with field stones. They had gathered split rails from a collapsed fence nearby to sit on and had already unpacked their canvas bags. Possum had placed his big coffee pot on the fire and had set out several half-gallon glass jars of food. Grandpa Windy pulled a large Ball canning jar out of his bag and said, "Brought some canned tenderloin." That got everybody's attention. Canned pork tenderloin!

In Hilltown we slaughtered hogs and other animals and salted the meat down in the smoke house or canned it in glass jars. Hams were usually smoked, shoulders and side meat were made into salted tenderloin, and other parts of the animal were canned for later.

It was generally accepted that there was nothing in this world as good as canned pork tenderloin, particularly my Granny Hill's.

Dollar brought a large basket of biscuits and several others brought skillets for cooking over the fire. Before long, the fall moon was shining brightly. The early November night was perfect for coon hunting. With coffee perking, pork tenderloin sizzling in one pan and biscuits warming in another, the smell of the cooking was overpowering. To me even the coffee smelled good. I'd never had it before.

The coon hounds tied to a fence about twenty yards away were getting restless—barking, snapping, straining on their leashes, howling ready for a hunt. I too wondered when the hunting would begin. About that time Windy said to Possum, "Let's turn 'em dogs loose." And they did.

These dogs were the pride and joy of their owners. The men fed them well; made sure they were healthy. A good coonhound came with bragging rights.

Windy was particularly proud of his Blue Tic hound. The story went that one day his first Blue Tic ran away or was taken by someone. Windy was in a real tizzy, until a few days later, a Blue Tic showed up at his place all covered with mud, smelling awful. That night Ne-nee and Windy gave the old dog a bath and spritzed on some of Granny's perfume to make him smell real good before locking him up in the dog lot, happy to have their hound back.

However, in the light of day they realized that they had babied the wrong Blue Tic. Windy said, "Shucks we've put all this into him, I'm going to keep this old dog if nobody comes for him." And no one ever came inquiring about a Blue Tic hound, so it became Windy's Blue Tic.

Originally enough, he named it "Blue Tic."

Blue Tic was with us this night and like the other dogs he was rarin' to go. When the men turned the hounds loose, they bounded across the fields and into the woods, barking, snapping and rushing to catch the first sent of a coon or a 'possum or even an unlucky cat.

Anything that could run and climb a tree was fair game. They had no interest in burrowing critters like fox or rabbit or a polecat. Those critters had their own dogs to contend with. Tonight was for coonhounds.

The elders listened carefully and claimed to know when the dogs were loafing, when they were following the scent of something, and when they had something treed by listening to the various barks. As I listed to a blow-by-blow account of these barking sounds first from Windy, then Possum and Dollar, I soon decided that I could tell the difference in the sounds of their barking as well.

As we all listened to our dogs, sipped coffee and ate tenderloin biscuits, we suddenly sensed that something was nearing our campsite. We could see an outline and ghostly shadows from the light of our fire. It appeared to be a man, a big towering man. A giant by Hilltown standards. Everyone tensed not knowing who or what it might be until Windy announced, "Hell, it's just Woody."

Woody? Why that was my daddy! He had come home and would now join our hunt. He declared the night to be just made for coon hunting, being so crisp and clear outside with a full moon. He wanted to be with us. Later, I came to believe differently. To leave work at seven in the evening, drive home over country roads and drop off several riders along the way only to arrive home after nine o'clock was a very full day. Why would anyone have been anxious to join a coon hunt? More than likely a worrying Momma had sent him to keep an eye on her boy.

Whatever the reason I was comforted and proud to have him along as we sat on the split rails and finished our meal of biscuits and tenderloin.

The tone of the barking dogs changed and Dollar jumped up, yelling, "They've treed something. It's a 'coon!" Windy, Possum, Roy and Daddy all stood and listened. They agreed that the dogs had treed something and we needed to go and find out what it was. So off we went, carrying lanterns, flashlights, and rifles as we enjoyed the last of the biscuits.

It wasn't long before we reached the place where the dogs circled and barked around a tree. But, just as we arrived the dogs broke off and fled hot on the trail of something else.

We turned our flashlights up the tree and the light gleamed on a set of eyes looking down at us. I could clearly see those eyes reflected in the light. Several of the men with their lights shining upward and their guns handy circled the tree for a better look. Then Roy said, "Damn it's a wild cat."

Dirty said, "Shoot it Daddy, shoot it."

Almost immediately, the .22 caliber single-shot rifle cracked and the cat tumbled down to the ground. I ran up and looked at it and it looked just like a house cat to me—maybe a house cat turned wild but no Wild Cat. Shucks!

Windy and Possum had not waited to shoot the cat. They followed the dogs, which had treed something else. The hounds were going wild, howling and barking at the foot of a large Sycamore tree. The older men said they were barking 'raccoon!'

We all left Roy to decide what to do with the cat and followed the sound of barking. The hounds had treed a 'coon.

Flashlight beams pinned the animal and Windy said, "Wade, come here so you can see him." Edging over to my Grandpa and looking up the beam of his flashlight I saw it. It sure was a raccoon. I not only saw its eyes but its natural black and white mask as it peered down and hissed at the dogs.

There was no hurry. The men with rifles circled the tree, talking to each other, measuring the raccoon in very descriptive terms. This was an important moment. Then Possum said, "Who's going to shoot this one?"

"Let's let Woody do it." Grandpa Windy spoke up, "He came in from work and came straight over here. We'll have other chances tonight. He's tired, Wade may want to walk him home before midnight and who knows how long we'll be here." Then Daddy took sharp aim with his rifle and with one *crack* brought the 'coon tumbling down. The dogs rushed forward not to eat it but to taste the smell of the animal. Daddy and Grandpa shooed them away before damage was done. Daddy held it up in the light of the flashlights and said, "Wade, what do you think of this?"

"Our first coon," I said. It was a scene I would not soon forget. That was our first coon. (Or at least, my first 'coon.)

Then the dogs bolted off through the fields and into the woods on with their hunt while we trudged back to the bonfire analyzing the happenings so far and the merits of the first raccoon caught this night.

Before much longer, Daddy stood and stretched and said, "Boys, I got up at four-thirty this morning and now it's near midnight. Wade's going to walk me home. I haven't had dinner yet."

Windy said, "Well, Wade's had a good night. He knows what coon huntin' is about now. We'll give you boys a report tomorrow;

but, don't expect it before afternoon because some of us won't be getting up so early tomorrow," he said looking at Ne-nee.

Daddy and I trudged back over the fields to our house. He carried the rifle and I carried the raccoon.

Just as we entered our property from the back side there was a long, mournful sound penetrating the clear moonlight night air. We stopped and listened for a minute. I said, "Daddy what is that?"

He paused for a minute, and then he said, "It's a huntin' horn, they're calling the dogs in. They may be home soon too."

"A huntin' horn?"

"Yep," Daddy said. "You know like the one Windy has hung by a leather strap beside the telephone in the pantry. The one made out of a bull's horn."

"Oh, yeah," I replied. But I had never heard a real one before. It sounded like those horns the Vikings used in the picture shows.

We slipped into the back door of our house and up the stairs with Daddy saying, "Let's be real quiet, and don't wake your Momma up."

After I went to bed, I could hear Momma talking to Daddy but I would have to wait 'til morning to find out what he was telling her. I was too tired to slip over to their closed door and listen, which I did from time to time. I thought, *Momma will tell me—if I need to know.*

And the skinning of that Coon would have to wait 'til morning too.

ODA: A Mother, A Grandmother

At times, a special relationship exists between a child and a grandparent, a relationship that is more than love and one that goes deep to their very souls. Because of their life experiences together, a spiritual understanding develops.

Such was my relationship with Daddy's mother, Oda Osborne Gilley. Oda was a woman of strong will, with opinions some say were shaped by her Western North Carolina mountains and Cherokee heritage. Our relationship developed during the turbulent years of World War II and lasted for more than thirty years. It was largely founded on lessons learned from the economic Depression of the 1930s, and though my relationship with Oda was different from that with Momma, it helped to guide me through a Hilltown childhood just as surely.

Oda Osborne Gilley had suffered much in her lifetime. She lost her mother while very young, was raised by an uncle, married an itinerant lumberman and tenant farmer younger than her, immediately had seven children and had to move them occasionally from job to job and place to place before she lost her husband in 1934 at the height of the Great Depression. She also suffered from a nutritional deficiency known as Pellagra, which was common in the South. For much of her adult life, even beyond when she had to, Oda kept to a rigid Pellagra diet, which landed her at the doctor's office with collapsed bowels after more than twenty years. Through all this, she remained as an oak, undaunted by it all.

Her life and lifestyle had given her a certain belief in the future and the hereafter. It was all very mystical to me, and I remember going to Hard Shell Baptist revivals and following her lead. The churches she attended tended to have service once a month, and it was an all day affair, including dinner. We did everything any church would do over the course of a week or month but all on one Sunday. Granny Oda took me to a couple of those, and while I was comfortable with her, I was not as comfortable at those gatherings.

But Oda's inner strength came from more than surviving hard times or being a Hard Shelled Baptist. It came from a deeper and more fundamental perception of the world and life, and when she turned to those depths, I as a young boy was… well, scared…. And I am reluctant to think of it even today. But that is another whole other story.

Lye Soap and Soap Operas

I walked to the door leading to the open air basement, or underhouse, of Granny Oda Gilley's Eagle Bottom house, looked around for a long, long minute, and then slammed the door shut, locking Granny, Pearl and Reba inside.

They all stopped talking and turned to look at the closed door. Reba said, "Wade, what do you think you are doing? What are you doing???"″

I peered in through the lattice that formed the walls of the ground level basement or under-house and storage room and laughed. I had caught them distracted and now they would play with me whether they wanted to or not.

Reba reacted immediately almost yelling, "Wade, you come here and unlock this door. Now! Right this minute!"

Peering through the lattice, excited because they were excited, full of my five years I replied, "Don't have the key. Ha, ha, ha, ha."

That was true, I didn't have the key to the lock, which had been hanging loose on the door while Granny Oda, my father's mother, and three of her daughters were making lye soap in a big black iron kettle hanging from the top of a tripod of iron rods over a hot wood fire in the yard on the north side of Granny's house.

ODA: A Mother, A Grandmother

Granny, Reba and Pearl had gone inside the open air basement to look at some glass jars and they were so totally engrossed in discussing the potential of those jars that they had not noticed me or thought about the possibilities of being locked in. Granny's other daughter, Ruby, (or Rube as we called her) had been sent to her house next door for some glass jars and was not present at the time I had locked the others in the basement room.

Granny was keeping me while Momma worked the day shift in the cotton mill. Rube's husband, Foy, and Pearl's husband, Doug, were both away in the U.S. Army at this time, and Russ, Granny's youngest son and my namesake, had just finished basic training and left for Europe a few days earlier as the Allies prepared for a major offensive against the Nazis. So the women had decided to make soap.

Making lye soap was not only cost effective but was a social thing in those days, as it was a time to work and wait and while waiting to talk and tell stories. In fact, lye soap making, an art in colonial days had been revived during the Great Depression. It cost much less for families with more time than money to make their own soap than to buy it from Proctor and Gamble. (Actually Mr. Proctor and Mr. Gamble had, almost a hundred years earlier, through their ingenuity and the marvels of the industrial revolution, made soap that was so inexpensive that most Americans bought rather than made their own soap after the 1850s, but during the War in hill country, it was well worth the effort.)

The making of lye soap was not easy. First the women had to get the ingredients, including lots of animal fat and the lye itself. Lye could be bought in most stores in tin cans, or it could be made at home by pouring water through wood ashes, which resulted in a highly acidic solution or lye. The lye was mixed with scraps of animal fat and skin left over from hog or cattle killing and placed in a large metal kettle over a fire outside. This mixture was cooked for some time until it formed soap. While the soap was being made, the women had sufficient idle time between the steps to gossip. Some people believe that soap making and the stories are directly associated with the name given to the new serialized radio programs of the 1930s known as "Soap Operas" or just "Soaps." I once read that, by 1940, more than forty percent of all adult women listed to these radio dramas or Soap Operas on almost a daily basis.

But today's 'soap opera' was going on in real time in Granny's open air basement, much to my delight. While Granny and two of her daughters were locked in the open air basement, their lye soap cooked, cooked and then over cooked. Before long there was a certain and distinctive smell coming from the boiling pot and the seriousness of the situation began to dawn on me.

This was trouble, big time.

Shortly though, Rube showed up and saw what was happening. She yelled at me, "Wade what did you do? Where is the key? You come here right nooow and help me"

Granny got Rube's attention and told her where to find the key inside the house. Almost immediately, she came bounding down the steps into the yard, grabbed the master lock and unlocked the basement door. Out burst Granny, Reba and Pearl all having unkind words and harsh looks for me. The three younger women hurried to the smoking soap while Granny turned to me and I could just tell what she was thinking. She grabbed a small tree branch lying on the ground near the kettle and started coming in my direction. She was fast for an old woman in an ankle length blue skirt and red sweater. She was mad. I turned and scampered away from my fifty three year old grandmother (53 sure looked old then) by running up the hillside toward Rube's house.

Rube's house was another six-room dwelling with two bedrooms upstairs, perched on a little hill just north of Granny's house. In between was a small branch, which became larger after each major rainfall and a ditch better known as a gully. I ran and ran and ran down into the gully and up the other side. But just as I started up the hill, my angry Granny caught me and I got one good whipping with that tree branch, a whipping I vividly remember sixty years later.

As Granny administered justice (her definition) she told me again and again why she was doing it. Then she marched me down the hillside back to her house as I cried and rubbed my eyes. For the rest of the afternoon, I sat on the front porch watching while the women cleaned up the mess and saved as much lye soap as possible. There was no going inside and no going down the stairs to the yard. There was no going anywhere that afternoon as per Granny's orders. Much later, after a day of being deliberately ignored by my aunts and grandmother, I was picked up by my mother. Granny met her car at the road and they had an extensive and intensive discussion with much hand waving by both women. I had really messed up, and now I was going to hear about it again and again. Momma was not one to let a guy forget a mistake. But all the way home, an automobile ride of some twenty minutes, she was very calm. She asked me lots of questions, but none that let to a discussion of the afternoon events. She would get to that in due time.

But strangely, Momma said nothing critical—on the way home or ever.

On arriving home that day we carried on as if nothing had ever happened. She just never brought the incident up. You see she respected Granny, but was independent and not one of Oda's (Granny Gilley) daughters and didn't defer to her. She was Forest Gladys Hill Gilley, first and foremost a Hill from Hilltown, and then, and only then, a Gilley. And in those parts a Hill didn't defer to anyone, especially a mother-in-law

Then, before I knew it, morning came again, and we were up bright and early at six o'clock eating breakfast before getting Momma's 1937 Chevrolet to drive to Granny's house for another long day while Momma worked in the mill. For obvious reasons, I was not terribly excited about what might happen that day at Granny's house. But when I arrived Granny was polite, if cool, and so it went for most of the morning. We just sat in the sitting room as she did some mending, looked at what was cooking on the wood stove and let me attempt to read those books Momma always seemed to have around for me and my idle time.

The day dragged on and on, and I became more and more bored. However, there was a certain uneasiness or tension in the air, or it seemed to me. That time I spent just sitting in that small room with Granny was in many ways more painful than the whipping

Granny Oda Gilley and her oldest daughter Belle Davenport in the 1950s.

ODA: A Mother, A Grandmother

I had experienced the previous afternoon and the d
move so slowly. The morning was endless.

Then, just before mid-day just at the time we wc
eat lunch, my Granny came in the living room, where I was sitting and reading a book, looked at me in her unique, intense and unforgiving way that was her and said, "Wade, would you like to have a picnic?"

This was unusual, for Granny never seemed to do anything just for fun or leisure. But having a picnic would sure be better than what we were doing, just sitting around the house with a tension in the air thick enough to be cut with a butter knife. So I said, with great and real enthusiasm, "Sure. Let's go." Then I asked, "Where are we going to have a picnic, Granny?"

"We'll go to the top of the hill," she said, pointing to the hill rising behind her house. At that point in my life, all five years of it, that hill seemed to be a mountain.

And so we picnicked. First, she packed a worn, woven wicker basket with food and other things needed for a picnic, then we climbed the hill that overlooked all of Eagle Bottom. It was one of the few times I ever climbed that hill and saw all of the Bottom in one perspective, even though I made many trips to that community over the years continuing through my high school days. It was a beautiful day in those Blue Ridge Mountains of Virginia and it seemed that we could see forever.

Granny stopped, spread out a blanket and sat down. Then she patted a spot on the blanket by her side with a dark and strong hand and said, "Come over here, Wade, and we'll eat."

I sat down with her, watching as she opened the basket and pulled out sliced tomatoes in wax paper and saltine crackers in their bag along with a quart jar of well water. We each ate several of the sandwiches—saltines with slices of tomato—while she explained what I had done that was so wrong the day before and why she had given me the whipping I had received. To hear it told from her perspective everything made perfect sense

I had gotten in trouble without knowing why and she had to make a point of it to teach me a life's lesson. It seemed that Granny's life mission was to teach hard lessons.

Before Sister

As we began to get ready to leave the hilltop, I edged closer and told her, "Granny Oda, I am so sorry for doing that. And I ran away because I was scared." This was not the first but rather one of many confessions I would give during the course of my life.

She didn't smile but now looking back, I realize there seemed to be a hint of humor in her voice and, maybe, just maybe, a sparkle in her eyes as she accepted my apology. I had done wrong and admitted it.

I was truly sorry, and she took my hand as we walked back down the hill together. We must've made quite a pair. She was a slim dark woman of some Cherokee decent, dressed in a long skirt hanging down to her shoe tops, with waist length hair tied up in a bun on the back of her head. Her stride even had a certain authority and her hand provided a strong, reassuring grip. Tightly holding on to Oda Davis Gilley's hand was a five year old, with light brown (piss burnt I later learned) hair, tall for his age, son of her first son and grandson of her husband who had died some ten years earlier. It was easy walking down that hill that day; in fact it was like walking on a cloud.

We had an understanding that would last forever

Kidnapping Rube and Reba Marries

"Your daddy did the right thing," Momma said. "Stay out of other people's business, and you'll be better off." She was commenting on what had occurred as we sat on our front porch that evening in about 1943. The three of us had been sitting there after supper when an old four door coupe came cruising down the dirt and gravel Hilltown road with dark blinds covering the two rear and back windows. I recognized it as Granny Gilley's car. The driver was Daddy's youngest brother, Russ, James Russell Gilley to be accurate. This was before Russ had slipped away from Granny, joining the Army sometime in 1943 only to be killed at the Battle of the Bulge in January, 1945.

The big brown touring car eased up to the side of the road near our mail box. Russ rolled the window down and said, "Wood, Mom

ODA: A Mother, A Grandmother 97

wants to talk with you." It seemed like forever before Daddy answered. He took several long puffs on his Camel cigarette, looking cool and detached. "What does she want?" he finally asked.

He knew well what was going on, for he and Momma had been talking about it for several days. Granny had taken (kidnapped Daddy later called it) her next to youngest daughter, Ruby, and was not allowing her to go back to her new husband Foy Phibbs. Granny was strongly set against marriage. Everyone thought it was due to her bitter experience of having birthed seven children, one right after the other before her husband, James Webb Gilley, had died from spinal meningitis related pneumonia in 1934. She was left with seven children at home having no good way to support them. She was very hard set against her girls marrying. So, when Rube ran away with her boy friend Foy to Sparta, North Carolina, I was told, (there was no waiting period or required blood tests over there) and got married, all hell had broken loose at Granny Oda's house. Foy, who would shortly be in the Army, was a local Fries boy and cotton mill worker.

Granny was surprised at their marrying because, even though Rube had gone to work in the cotton mill, Oda didn't suspect that she was seriously dating, much less thinking about getting married. As soon as Granny learned of this carrying on (her words) she made a point of confronting Foy and Rube on the matter. Getting nowhere she took Rube straight home to Eagle Bottom Road, and locked her in her room.

A drama had played out in the front yard of Granny's house that morning and had been something of a standoff. Granny gave no ground, and Foy ended up not seeing his wife for a couple of days. The back and forth anguish had been going on without resolution when the old touring car came cruising down Hilltown Road with Granny and Rube concealed in the back seat behind the dark window shades. From outside the car, no one could see the backseat occupants. But Russ was apparent at the steering wheel of the coupe wearing a short billed cap placed jauntily on the side of his head, smoking a Camel cigarette. It was obvious that he wanted help from his older brother. Like Wood, Russ was not one to enjoy these domestic disputes, but he followed Granny's orders—at times.

"Wood, Mom said for you to come down here and git in. She wants to talk with you."

"Nope, that's none of my business," was Daddy's reply.

Russ looked both anxious and irritated. He turned and talked for a minute with someone in the darkened back seat before saying, "Hey Wood, I told you Mom needs you. Now!"

"I guess you all do need help, but I can't provide it. Y'all have work this out with them (Foy and Rube)."

At that Russ became more irritated. After turning for another conversation with the backseat, he flicked his cigarette out the window, pulled his hat down straight over his head and, while looking angrily at Daddy, drove off. I could have sworn that he gave Daddy the finger, even though no one said anything.

As it was growing darker, we picked up our stuff off the front porch and went inside to go to bed. Not one word was said about what had just happened except, as she was tucking me in bed, Momma said, "Your Daddy was right. Keep your nose out of other folks' business."

The next I heard of this affair was the following night when the telephone rang during supper—two shorts and a long—and Daddy jumped up and ran to get the phone. He stayed on the line for several minutes as Momma and I continued to eat our supper. He mostly was listening, except for a few short questions. After he came back to the table and sat down to finish his supper, Momma picked up our plates, and we watched him slowly, deliberately eat his supper. He volunteered no commentary, and Momma was fit to be tied. She restrained herself, however.

"Well?" She said after the longest time.

"Well what?" Daddy retorted.

"Well, What happened?"

"Well, he got his dander up and went to see Bruce Smith to inquire as to what could be done."

"Oh?"

"Yep. Mom finally told them she would think about it. And she did, because Rube is now back with Foy."

Blonde beauties Reba and Ruby Gilley in Eagle Bottom in the early 1940s.

"Oda just gave in?"

"Well… no she worked it out."

"A deal?"

"Yeah, Mom thought about the situation and she, Rube and Foy talked it out."

"What did they decide?"

"As I understand it, from Pearl, who was just on the phone, Mom said that she would let Rube go back to him if they would do one thing. And they agreed to do it."

"One thing? Well what was that?"

"Mom had learned that a house next to hers, the one built on the little knoll, was going to be for rent. She said that if Foy and Rube rented it instead of living down in Fries, she would give in to the marriage. She wouldn't have it annulled, as if she could have." Daddy shrugged. "So, They agreed, they will move to Eagle Bottom and live next door to Mom."

With Pearl living just up the road and Ruby moving in next door, Granny would still have her three youngest girls living right there with her. So, that was the compromise for that day. But, there must have been more to the solution, as Foy and Rube followed Granny every time she moved after that day. When Daddy built Granny a new house in Hawkstown, the Phibbs soon built themselves a house on the lot next door to hers. Then they moved to Smyth Country with her some ten years later buying a farm just up the road from Oda. (In 2002 they had been happily married more than fifty five years.)

"So, Granny really won?" Momma said.

"She usually does, but sometimes you have to let her figure it out for herself," Daddy responded.

That night, as Momma was tucking me in the bed, she said, "You see, Wade? I told you. Keep your nose out of other's business, and they will figure it out for themselves."

That wasn't the last time that Granny had a fit when one of her girls got it in her head that she wanted to get married. Bell was first, and seemingly out foxed Granny, when she married Henry Davenport just before Granny and the rest of the family moved to Fries in about 1935. Pearl, being as strong willed as Granny herself, soon married Doug Lambert of Fries with little fanfare. However, the two youngest girls had more of a struggle.

For example, it was not that long after Rube married that beautiful baby girl Reba, who was then working in the cotton mill herself, began looking around at the guys. Her first boyfriend, named Sam, though friendly with Daddy, was definitely not acceptable to Granny—not that anyone would have been. Another boyfriend who showed up shortly was a mild mannered man from the Hawkstown area, Bernard "Rabbit" Hawks. He later worked at the Radford Arsenal until his retirement, where Daddy worked for so long and retired as well.

Daddy liked Rabbit from the git go, and it showed when Rabbit and Reba took their little trip and came home married. This time Granny was really in a quandary since Reba didn't plan on moving away from home. She came back home married and planned to spend time with her new husband on his four day weekends—a normal work week at the Arsenal, where people worked seven days and were off four. This was different. There was no need to kidnap Reba, she was already home. So, what was Granny to do? She took to her bed, moaning and groaning, carrying on like she was going to die. When anyone tried to pacify her, she would moan and talk she was dying. The situation got totally out of control, so the girls again turned to their older brother, Woodrow.

That was on a Saturday morning, and Daddy thought about it all day. About five o'clock in the afternoon, he shaved and dressed in his Sunday best—a suit and tie (his one and only) and his narrow brimmed Stetson hat. I remember seeing Daddy look in the mirror, making sure every thing looked okay. He straightened his hat and tie, went out and left in his car –heading to Granny's.

Momma, my sister and I, were left sitting at home, wondering what was going on. I asked, "Well, what is he going to do?"

"Don't know," Momma said, "but I hope it's the right thing. He ought to mind his own business"

We later heard, from him, that he arrived at Granny's house, marched straight into her bedroom with his coat, tie and Stetson hat, and addressed the body lying in the bed moaning. He told her exactly what he thought. "Reba is a grown woman and needs a chance to live a life of her own. She's not running away, and she will always be there for you, Mom. You'll just have to get over this."

This direct approach and the realization that her plan wasn't working, apparently so shook up Granny that she rethought her whole strategy lying there in bed while he was talking.

"Wood, if that is all you have to say, git out of here so I can git up and git dressed," she said.

He left the room. As he and Reba sat looking at each other, out came Granny all dressed and ready to go. "Wood, make yourself useful. I'm going to Pearl's, and you're driving me." So, off they went, with everyone then wondering what would happen next.

Granny spent the night with Pearl and Doug and their 1945 blessing, a son named Jimmy (no nickname that I know of). Shortly she purchased a three-room house next door to Pearl, right there in Eagle Bottom. This act was totally unexpected and threw the entire family for a loop. What was she doing now? Negotiations had taken a new turn for the Gilley clan. Granny returned to her house and moved enough stuff to set up housekeeping in the new smaller house. Further negotiations began in earnest.

In the end, it was decided that Granny would return to her home in Hawkstown, and Reba and Rabbit would buy the cute little house next to Pearl for their own. And that was the way it worked for some time, as Granny came to accept Rabbit.

Later, after moving to Smyth County in 1958, the two households were consolidated into one in a large white farm house that Granny Oda bought. Rabbit continued to stay in a Radford area rooming house (later his own ranch style house) during the long work week and traveled home in Smyth County to be with Reba and Granny when he was off. They were all satisfied with that arrangement—or appeared to be.

Years later, remembering the two separate incidents, I asked Momma, "Did Daddy do the right thing when he dressed up and told Granny off?"

She thought for a minute and said, "Yes, I think he did the

right thing since you could never guess what that Oda might do. I'm just glad about the way it all turned out for Ruby and Reba. They're both good girls." (And beautiful too as one can see from their picture.)

Momma revisited those two incidents several times with me, often talking out loud, first on one side and then on the other. When it came to the relationships within the Gilley family, Momma was certain of some things, but she always minded "her own business." But Daddy liked to tell me those stories and I hope he didn't embellish them for my sake.

ODA's Way

"You'd be better off buying a farm than going to college," Granny said as we sat on her front porch in Hawkstown. I was close to graduating from Fries High School and had been admitted to VPI for the fall quarter. In a few days I would be heading to Richmond with several Hill cousins to work for the summer as an iron worker on the construction of the Richmond-Petersburg Turnpike.

"Why would you say that, Granny?" I asked.

"Your Daddy and Momma are going to pay all that money and at the end you won't have any property," she replied. "You buy a farm and get it paid for and it'll take you through any depression. If Webb had a farm we wouldn't have had such a hard time during the depression."

"But Granny, I ain't no farmer," I tried to tell her.

"No you ain't, you're just like your daddy. You want to go off and do something. That's why we differed," she related. Actually, I knew that they differed on many things, but if ever there were two people who understood one another it was Oda and Daddy.

"Some day you'll wish that you listened to me. Some day you'll wish you had a farm to fall back on," Granny said as that conversation ended. Little did I know that she was in the process of buying a beautiful farm in Smyth County and relocating half her family back to the place they had left during the Great Depression. They'd left the Washington County farm as tenant farmers to go to Fries so the kids could work in the cotton mill to support Granny and themselves. Now she was going back as the owner.

Two months later, she revisited the topic in another way. "Wish you'd leave that Smith girl alone," she said suddenly. "Wish that job in Richmond had worked out and you'd stayed and made some money like you told me you hoped to do."

"Me too, Granny. Me too. If I had been able to work more than two days a week I could've saved enough money to pay my first year in college," I replied, trying to divert her. Knowing Granny's distaste for girlfriends, I sure didn't want to go down that path.

But she did. "I know you're short on money but why did you come back and start running around with that girl again?" she said. I was having trouble following her. Why was she mixing two very different things here? Were we talking about school or women?

"What do you mean? I asked.

"Well, you were supposed to go to Richmond and work hard all summer and make money to help your daddy send you to college. Then that Smith girl didn't want you to go and y'all fell out, kinda broke up, right?" Granny continued. She obviously was going somewhere but where? "Now, you're back home, no money and running around with the girl again, that's what I hear. That right?"

Well she had it kinda right but what was the issue? I didn't come home early because of the girl, but because I lost the union job. Things had tightened up and the union was sending out iron workers with seniority and that didn't include guys who had just graduated from high school. I didn't come back home just to date a girl.

"I think you ought to run away from her. No more this dating, or whatever it is, that's what I think." Granny offered her advice in that direct way of hers.

It was quiet for moments that seemed like minutes. What was I to say? Finally, I responded, "Well Granny, I don't see the connection. I'm going to college in September. It's all set. Momma has already paid my tuition and Coach Moseley down at VPI has invited me to join the football team. Everybody knows that. That's set. Just dating some has nothing to do with that."

"Well, I've seen it happen. You kids do crazy things when it comes to women and the women are just as strong headed. I had trouble with some of mine," she continued. "First thing I know you'll be running off with a girl and your college dreams will be over. Reba told me about what happened to several of these Fries boys. Got girls in trouble and then they were working in the cotton mill for the rest of their lives."

So that was it. Her first preference for me was farming but college was better than getting married too early, or at all.

"Oh, Granny that's not going to happen, you'll see," I responded.

"Well, I want to make sure," she stated in very businesslike terms. Maybe it was business but what business? "What were you making down in Richmond?"

"In money? Not much," I confessed, "just enough to pay the boarding house and a little more. I brought forty dollars home."

"I mean how much would you've made if you had worked full time? I mean how much would you brought home a week, after everything?"

"Well if I could have worked as much as Junebug said when we left, I could have saved maybe fifty dollars a week. Maybe I could've saved five hundred dollars for the summer."

She sat and thought a for awhile and then said, "Tell you what. If you stop going around with that girl, I'll pay you thirty dollars a week for the rest of the summer"

Thirty dollars, I thought to myself. Thirty times six weeks would be a good sum, almost two hundred dollars. Besides, things were not going so well on the dating front as 'that girl' was going to South Carolina and said she might not come back to Fries and continue in high school. It would be easier than pie to avoid 'running around' with a girl who wasn't in town. (Granny occasionally confused running around with fooling around.)

But I couldn't not tell Granny, could I?

So I said, "Granny I don't think she's going to be around too much. She's going to South Carolina to be with her sister."

"No matter. For the rest of the summer I'll pay you thirty dollars a week and you'll use that to help your daddy pay your college bills." I didn't mention that Momma had saved for four years working in the cotton mill and she had $1300 for me, enough to pay for two years. Maybe Granny knew, 'cause she always seemed to know things.

"Well let me see," I said.

The next night, sitting on the front porch at the Smith's I told the young lady what Granny had proposed. She listed for several minutes and then became angry, "You had that discussion with her? About me and you? Some kind of deal?" And then she stood up and marched into the house and shut the front door.

The next day, I stopped by Granny's and told her what had happened. She listened then said, "Looks like you're going to earn your thirty dollars this week," she said and handed me an envelope of cash that I gave to Momma.

I got another envelope the next week, but the third week when I stopped by she said, "Reba told me that you were right."

"Right about what, Granny?"

"That girl has gone to South Carolina."

"Well, I told you she might," I responded.

"Well, she's gone and our deal is off, you knew she was leaving. You didn't have to do anything," Granny concluded the discussion on that subject forever. However, I later learned from Daddy that she gave him some money to give me for spending and things. And I needed it. Daddy said that even though I might have known the girl was leaving Granny still felt she had intervened at the right moment and forced the issue. Maybe she did. Maybe she didn't, who knows?

Oda could be scary too. Oh everyone knew that she wanted to have her way and she always had her way for everything. But that wasn't the scary part.

Once when I was ten or so I found myself sitting on that same front porch listening to Granny. She was talking to me giving my Daddy the devil, or so it seemed to me. I was very sensitive to criticism of Daddy from anybody except Momma. (Momma could do no wrong in those years.) At this time, according to Granny, he wasn't doing things the way she wanted and this talk went on forever it seemed. Or it went on until I had had enough and spoke up, "I'm lucky to have Daddy and you're lucky to have him too," I boldly stated.

That hit her hard. Not too many talked back to her, certainly not a small grandson in his bib overalls sitting on her front porch. She snapped something at me and to my surprise then and now I took up for myself and Daddy saying, "Momma told me."

Her eyes narrowed and I could see them like bright beans under the brim of her straw hat. She just stared forever it seemed and I got real nervous wishing I had not gone down that path. Momma had told me, "Don't try to tell Granny something she don't want to hear." Daddy had said, "no matter what she says respect your Granny."

Then she said, "Come here. Sit here beside me!"

It was a command and even if I didn't want to I knew I had to. So after a few minutes I got up and sort of side stepped over and sat beside Granny.

She said, "Look at me boy. What has your Momma been telling you?"

I looked and blurted out, "She said you wanted to name me Webb (after my grandfather James Webb Gilley) but she stopped that and named me Wade."

That set Granny back a step and right away, I wished I had kept my mouth shut. Then she reached out and took my face in both her hands and pulled me to her to the point all I could see were those eyes looking straight into mine. She wouldn't let me move and we just kept looking into each other's eyes for the longest time. It seemed forever. How I wished Momma would come for me now.

Then she said, "You know that you are named for me, don't you?" I squirmed and she continued, "I am Oda. Oda is an old, old name and you are W'Oda or son of Oda. Did she tell you that?" How could that be? No one had ever told me anything like that. I was scared. "You are the one," she continued. "You are W'Oda. You always remember that boy. I am 'Oda' and you are 'W'Oda'. We will always be Oda and W'Oda. No matter what."

It was not necessarily the words but the look in her eyes that seemed to pierce my soul. It took several days before I got up the nerve to ask Momma about the name. She looked at me and sort of laughed and said, "I named you after the guy in Gone With the Wind. I did it. Woodrow wanted to name you exactly for his daddy but I named you. Don't you ever forget that." Then she added, "Those Cherokee girls from North Carolina are always talking like that".

What a relief. Wow! Momma told me exactly what I needed to start sleeping at night again.

But years went by and things happened and I wondered. Wade, or W'Oda?

Oh No Not Russ!

A dark greenish car pulled into Granny Oda's driveway, and two men in brown military uniforms got out, stretched, carefully straightened their coats and short brimmed army caps, and started toward the front door. It was January, 1945, and I was staying the day with my Granny Gilley while Momma worked in the Fries cotton mill. Granny Oda got up from the living room chair and slowly walked to the window, shading her eyes with her hand. I peeped out the window below from behind her flowing skirts.

As the two army officers walked upon the front porch and began to knock, Granny turned back to the room and started screaming "Oh, oh, no! Oh, nooooooooo. Not Russ!" She started flailing around, seemingly fighting something unseen. She yanked her hair down. The long, below the waist length bun on the back of her head now flowed down, covering her whole upper body, including most of her face. She sat in the floor. Her face contorted. Tears rolled down her cheeks. She flung her glasses across the room. She was out of control—an unusual phenomenon for her. This was news she had been expecting... and dreading for months. I was stunned for I had never seen a grown up fall apart like that—it was frightening, I didn't know what had happened to Granny.

I ran past her to the door and let the officers in the house. They rushed to where Granny was lying and lifted her up onto

ODA: A Mother, A Grandmother

the sofa. With their hats in their hands, the two officers attempted to console her.

She said, "It's Russ, ain't it? It's my baby boy. He's gone. I told him, told him. He won't listen. He won't listen...."

She was right. These men were carrying the official notice that Oda Davis Gilley's youngest child, James Russell Gilley, my partial namesake, had been fatally wounded at a place named Elsenborn Ridge in Belgium. He had succumbed in the largest land battle of World War II— the Battle of the Bulge.

Most Americans today do not realize that world freedom hung in the balance in December of 1944 and January of 1945, and that the major German counterattack through Belgium almost succeeded. But in the end, gallant Americans and other Allies turned them back. The Battle of the Bulge was the largest land battle of all time. 600,000 Allied troops were involved with more than 80,000 casualties for the Americans alone—some 19,000 were killed, including James Russell Gilley. (Actually, Russ' legal name was Russell James Gilley because, like my daddy, he had legally reversed his two given names but Granny never recognized the change.) Daddy was named Charles Woodrow Gilley, for his uncle Charles who was gassed in World War I, and Woodrow, for President Woodrow Wilson. Wilson had sent Uncle Charles on what some thought was a useless loss of American lives, refereeing a quarrel between the English and Germans. But Daddy was high on President Wilson, a Democrat, and since everyone called him Woodrow anyway, he went to the courthouse and had his name changed to Woodrow Charles or WC to some.

Later, when I was a college teacher and administrator in the 1960s and 1970s, I found that my students were always surprised that almost as many casualties occurred over a two-month period around the Battle of the Bulge as was experienced in the six years of the Vietnam War or the five years of the Korean War. They were equally surprised to learn that the average age of those dying in the two-month battle for democracy was just over twenty, the average age of the typical undergraduate student then and today.

Granny Gilley didn't know all this either. All she knew was

that her baby boy, barely twenty-one, was dead. Russ was initially buried in Belgium, but he was disinterred in 1947 and brought back to be reburied in Grayson County, Virginia where Granny planned to be buried. I remember that funeral, especially the extreme emotions it brought to our family. While many families in Fries and surrounding communities had loved ones in the Army, only a few actually lost a son. While many went, I don't remember many coming back in boxes.

Later, standing at the graveside as they buried Russ up in Grayson County after bringing him back from Belgium, I reflected on my personal memories of my namesake and uncle.

One memory of Russ was in late 1943 or early 1944 when he was home for the last time before shipping out for Europe. All of Oda Gilley's family had gathered at Ruby's house in Eagle Bottom for dinner and something of a going away party—a goodbye. I remember seeing him leaning against the doorframe, dressed in his brown army uniform. Russ was a tall, easygoing person. His hat was cocked on the side of his head, and he puffed on his ever present Camel Cigarette.

No one there knew this would be the last night any of his family would ever see him alive. They were all just enjoying these moments of being with him but there was a tenseness in the air. After all things were heating up in Europe but that was something I understood little about. I was just glad to see Russ.

I also remember how everything was rationed during the war years, and that it was almost impossible to buy candy and other non-essentials. Everything was needed for the war effort. The only way to get gasoline stamps was to prove it was needed for the war effort.

However, we had candy bars when most of my Hilltown cousins did not. Russ sent his monthly army allocation to his mother, who carefully parceled it out. That was my first memory of Baby Ruth bars, with their peanuts and gooey Carmel. Soooo good! That is, in reality, my first memory of real candy bars, because of the rationing had started when I was so young. Granny was careful to see that this gift from Russ was fairly distributed among all of

ODA: A Mother, A Grandmother 111

Gramma Oda at Russ's grave stone at Saddle Creek Cemetery about 1960.

us, and she rarely took any for herself. Her gift was knowing that Russ was still alive.

Then he wasn't, and the rest of the war was a blur to us.

The war ended. Soldiers, for the most part, came home to celebrations. Russ' loss was a shadow that hovered over the Gilleys for some years. Of course, a new generation lived. My sister Mickey was born, along with cousins Jimmy Lambert (Aunt Pearl's son), and Gary "Teek" Phibbs (Aunt Ruby's son). The economy changed. Daddy went into the trucking business, only to go broke. The time came and went, but Russ' death continued to haunt us all.

In 1947, the long awaited event arrived. Russ was finally coming home from Europe. Granny had the choice to bring him home or leave him undisturbed, but she wanted the two of them to be together once again. She had bought two grave sites at Saddle Creek Church in Grayson County. People thought that she would move her husband from his resting place in North Carolina to be with her. In the end, though, it was just Russ and she buried together. She never forget that she could have prevented his enlistment for a while thus taking some personal responsibility for his fate..

The funeral was emotional, but what my father went through before was even more so. Oda wanted to know for sure that it was Russ that they were bringing home after almost two years in the ground in Belgium, so she said, "Woodrow, you'll have to go and see him and then tell me."

And he did. But for some reason, he took me with him to the funeral home for the viewing. I don't think he expected that I would participate, but I was along to observe my daddy. Maybe that was why I was there? While Daddy was unnerved by the viewing, I believe he knew it was Russ. In the car he turned and said to me—a nine year-old boy—"It's Russ." It was as though he was reassuring us both that it was his baby brother's body.

In time, things improved. Daddy went to work at the Radford Arsenal, and Granny, along with Reba and "Rabbit", Ruby, Foy and Teek, moved back to Smyth County, near where everything had begun, at least in Granny's mind. Still it would never be as it once was.

And I shall never forget that she lost Russ, the love of her life, that she persevered so well for so long, and that she was an inspiration for more than a few of us.

My last memory of Oda was from 1971, when she lay on her death bed near Chilhowie, Virginia in her Smyth County home. I presented my six month-old son to her as I had been presented to my great grandmother, Martha Jane, some thirty years before. Oda was not considered to be able to conduct a coherent conversation, having been bed ridden for some months, but Reba said, "We'll hold him up so that she can see him, and he can see her."

Unexpectedly, when presented with the boy, she focused and said something, which surprised everyone. She rarely said anything those days, so we were all excited. I said, "Reb, what did she say?"

Reba, the blonde beauty, the baby girl of that family about which Granny's latter life had revolved, turned with a strange look on her face and said, "Why, Why she said, 'White headed, just like my boys.' Can you believe that?"

I couldn't, but then again I could, knowing her inner strength.

Oda was still with us. Always will be, her and Russ.

Momma Gets Her Wishes

1945 was a year of change. Daddy's youngest brother Russ was killed at the Battle of the Bulge in January. Germany gave its statement of surrender on May 7. And on August 14, just one day before my seventh birthday, in those hazy days when real summer finally reached Virginia's Blue Ridge Mountains and Ne-nee and I were going about in our bare feet, Japan surrendered at last.

The fall brought even more change. In September, I was finally allowed to enter the first grade. In October, Sister was born and my relationship with my mother changed forever.

Getting me into school was a very big deal, because Momma had been trying to start me in school for the past two years. In 1943 she tried, but no one was going to let a five year-old start in the first grade back then. Then the previous September she had attempted to enroll me as a first grader at the Vaughan School, a Carroll County school about two miles from our home in the direction of Ivanhoe. However, due to strict enforcement of the Carroll County attendance and age rules, and overcrowded conditions plus interference of a cousin by marriage, Virgie Akers, I was rejected after two weeks in spite all of Momma's efforts. She thought I was ready and needed to be in school, but Virgie's plainly vindictive complaints prevented me from attending that year.

That battle with Virgie gave me my first insight into how mean some people can be mean just to be mean. None of her children ever finished elementary school, so it wasn't the quality of education that she was worried about when she complained about my age and got me blocked from first grade in 1944. It was just pure nastiness on her part. Somehow, she'd rather put my momma's children down than raise hers up.

But the situation was different in 1945. Because of overcrowding at Vaughan's tiny one-room school, I was assigned to the urban, well-organized, cutting edge Fries School. This should have been a wonderful thing. It wasn't always.

"Whap. Whap. Whap."

My bottom stung every time the paddle landed. Miss Slemp was administering the paddling, while saying, "Wade Gilley, I have told you time and again to stop talking. Now, I hope you understand that you have to be quiet and listen."

What I did to earn that paddling I shall never know, but Miss Slemp, an old maid and sister-in-law to assistant school principal Cy Bottoms, was definitive in her administration of discipline, and she made her point that day. I carefully avoided her wrath the rest of that entire year. It was not an easy first year of school, even though I could already read when most of the kids didn't even know their ABCs. However that was the year that I began to learn how tough teachers could and had to be to survive.

In 1945, the post war boom seemed to have arrived early in Fries. All the schools were crowded. The cotton mill and other industries started churning out domestic products for a goods-starved America. At the Fries elementary school, the first graders went to school in two shifts—morning and afternoon—because there were so many of us. I was placed in the morning shift, which meant that I attended class from about eight in the morning until noon. Then, Miss Slemp had another full class of first graders in the afternoon.

In later, wiser years I would come to understand that poor, overworked Miss Slemp had a very good reason for her 'paddle first and ask questions second' attitude. Fifty first graders a day would send anyone screaming for cover and she did the best she could to keep order

Those kids living in the independent fiefdom of Fries were usually dropped off by parents just minutes before their scheduled class and picked up soon after it was over. But, outsiders, like those of us from Hilltown, had two choices. Either our parents could drop us off and pick us up, or we could ride the school bus. If we took the bus, it meant spending the half-day we weren't in class in the Fries School auditorium under limited supervision.

I took the bus. I usually had a bag lunch, which I ate in the auditorium while I waited for the afternoon school bus. The afternoons were long and boring, and there were lots of opportunities to earn paddlings. I earned my fair share of them, and thought for a long time that Miss Slemp had something against me. Later in life while in education myself; I gained a greater appreciation for the challenges faced by teachers like Miss Slemp.

On one occasion, my first cousin Rex Gilley, who was in the third grade at Fries school, invited me to bring my bag lunch and come eat with him. Just after the lunch hour started, he came by the auditorium and we snuck out. He led the way up Sutphin Holler, past the old pre-prohibition saloon, and turned up the hillside through the laurel bushes. Under a grove of tall white pine trees, we lay back on the pine needle-carpeted woods and shared baloney sandwiches and peanut butter crackers. It was my favorite memory of Fries—sharing lunch with Rex under the pines. A week later, Rex's family pulled up stakes and moved to Portland, Oregon. I didn't see him again until we both had graduated from college, but in all that time I never forgot our lunch.

I also never forgot what followed that lunch. Rex walked back to school and was only a few minutes late for his third grade class, which was an all day affair. But I decided to walk home. For me, the walk to Hilltown was nothing. It was less than half the journey Ne-nee and I took each Saturday to go to the picture shows. But it took me most of the afternoon to make the journey, and the school bus arrived at our house before I did, which only made the problem worse.

When I missed the afternoon roll call at the school auditorium, Mr. Bottoms called my momma. At the time, though I had failed to realize it, she was very pregnant with my sister, which only added to the pandemonium that followed. Momma panicked and called Daddy. He came home early and went to Fries, looking for me. The school bus came and went. Finally, I showed up on the front porch and got such a grilling by Daddy that I've never forgotten it to this day.

I learned lots that first school year. I learned mostly that I was not living in a world of my own (or mine and Momma's). Teachers were in charge and had to be accommodated. My world was larger for just a little dalliance on the way home from a bag lunch with Rex, which set forces in motion that called me to account in a way that Momma had never done. And I learned how much Momma was willing to delegate to my teachers as she told Miss Slemp, and others later, "Paddle him every time he needs it and we'll give him one when he comes home."

Then one day in mid October that year, Miss Slemp came over to me and said, "Wade, your daddy is picking you up today. He is meeting you in front of the school building." So when the hour came, I grabbed my brown paper lunch bag and my book bag and ran out the door. I jumped in Daddy's car, and together we rode off. I sensed that something was happening, for he had never picked up before. But I was so happy to see him that I never thought to ask why he was picking me up.

"Go ahead and eat your lunch," Daddy said as he drove, not home but down toward Blair Town, and a small private community just east of Fries.

Eating my usual baloney sandwich and drinking the Coke that Daddy shared with me, I didn't pay attention to where we were driving and what we were doing at first. But after stopping at the third grocery store I asked, "Daddy, why do we need a whole case of Karo Syrup?" After all, I had never seen more than one bottle of it at home at a time. It was good on biscuits and pancakes, but why did he want a whole case?

He mumbled something, putting me off. Finally, when we were at Mr. Porter's grocery store in Stevens Creek, continuing to search for a case of Karo Syrup, he gave in to my questioning.

"Wade," he said, "you know that Aubrey has as baby brother—Tab?

"Yes."

"That Knotty has a baby sister—Gander?"

"Yes."

"You remember how much you talked about having a baby at our house?"

"Sure, Daddy. I remember. You promised me we would have a baby someday."

He paused and took a deep puff of his Camel cigarette, "Well Wade, your momma got us a baby sister today. What do you think about that?"

Think about that... think about that? Wow! I was catching up. Everybody I knew had a baby sister or a baby brother. This meant that we would be a regular Hilltown family now. It was exciting news. I bounced up and down and tried to hustle Daddy out of the store.

I could hardly wait to get home. After two more stops at stores we finally found the case of Karo, and sped home. I bounded up the front steps to the house and through the front door, only to stop and approach the sitting room quietly and with respect. My mother lay on the daybed. Her mother stood near the window holding a baby in her arms. Like me, Sister was delivered at home by Dr. Cox. Most babies in those days were delivered by house calling doctors, but several of my cousins born in the 1930s had been delivered at home by their grandmothers.

I approached the daybed, and Momma reached out and took my hands. She pulled me close and said, "Wade, You finally have that baby you've been wanting." She was happy—you could tell from the sparkle in her eyes. Daddy was smiling big, and I was excited for the arrival of Sister. (I didn't know it at the time but this was a big event and a turning point in my life, particularly in my relationship with my mother.)

That night was filled with even more excitement. Relatives came to visit. Kids came with their parents. Everyone brought food. It seemed all of Hilltown was excited by this event.

By the time it was dark, most of the company was gone. The dishes and pots and pans had been washed and put up. It was time to go to bed. Daddy was very careful to make sure everything was in order before he and I went upstairs to sleep. He tucked Momma in and told her to call him if she needed anything. He prepared a bottle, using some of that Karo syrup for Sister's feeding during the night.

Then we went up to bed. While I had slept with Momma lots, it was a rare treat for me to sleep with Daddy.

During the middle of the night I awoke with my bladder full to bursting. When Momma and I slept together, we just used the slop jar. But Daddy didn't go for that, so we walked down the stairs through the sitting room and kitchen to the back porch and urinated off the porch steps. We played a little game of seeing who could pee furthest out in the yard.

Then, in our under-shorts, we crept back through the house to where Momma and Sister were sleeping. A small night lamp was giving off light, creating shadows and outlining the two members of our family who were in the bed. We stopped and looked through the double-wide door.

Daddy said with obvious pride, "Well, Wade there they are. You've got your sister now."

"Yep," I responded, "we're a family now."

I thought, *Momma is happy*. And that's all that mattered.

Growing-Up Pains

As anyone who has or has been a child knows, growing up is not easy. Every generation looks back and says it is tougher now. Growing up in Hilltown in the 1940s and 1950s was both a challenge and a growing experience. Momma gave me room to spread my wings but she was always there for me.

The Best Five Dollars Ever Spent

We walked out of the Carroll County Courthouse in Hillsville, Virginia that bright and colorful October Monday in 1949 and Momma, standing by our car, flashed her broadest smile and remarked, "That was the best damn five dollars I ever spent!"

She seemed to be feeling good although she had just been fined five dollars, plus four dollars and ninety-five cents court costs (the minimum) by a frowning Judge Jack Mathews for threatening our neighbor and relative by marriage, Virgie Akers. While the judge had found Momma guilty of threatening Virgie, he had reduced her fine to five dollars and then given Virgie a lecture like nothing I have heard since, declaring, "I don't want to see this case here again or any cases like it. Do you understand, Mrs. Akers? If I do there will be more than one person fined. You folks have to learn to live together. Do you understand Mrs. Akers? Do you?"

What Momma had done was come to my defense and rescue on an October evening in 1949 when Virgie's two boys and a friend had ambushed me as I rode past the roadside garage of our neighbor and relative Ed "Jitney" Funk. They had knocked me off my bicycle, grabbed it and quickly locked it in the woodshed beside the garage. They refused to give it back as though they had some right to keep it. I had insisted that they give it back, and we ended up in a scuffle with Virgie coming out and egging her boys on, urging them to beat me up. She was a very threatening woman.

Seeing what had happened, four-year-old Sister had run up our front walk yelling and telling our Momma what was going on. It was then that Momma came to my rescue, using strong words that she would never repent—even though it later cost her five dollars.

This story really began when my father bought ten acres of land on the west end of Hilltown Road to build his and my mother's dream house. It was their dream, and as it turned out, others' irritation. During 1947 and into '48 he, with lots of help from expert workers and members of the family, constructed the finest house in all Hilltown. It had four rooms and a bath downstairs, three what then seemed to be large bedrooms upstairs and a full basement. It was brick, done in a modified Cape Cod style and was the first house in the community with an inside bathroom, even though that bathroom was not finished until a year after we moved in. It was the talk of Hilltown.

Daddy built a white picket fence all around a half-acre yard, connecting the brick arched entry gate from the main road with two other picketed gates into a handsomely enclosed front yard. Eventually the property had a good-sized garden, a two-acre alfalfa field, a two-story barn painted red, a hog pen and about three acres for grazing our milk cow, and for a short while, a small pony. (Actually, he had a deal with Leff Carico, another great-uncle by marriage and related through adoption to the neighboring William She'dan Carico, to lease grazing right to more than 20 acres behind our small farm and stretching all the way to the New River at Double Shoals, just above Fries Junction.)

The arched entrance to the yard and the stone walkway from the road up to the front porch is still there today just like Daddy built them.

Needless to say, that house was the pride—and the envy—of all Hilltown in those days and remains the largest and best built house there more than 40 years later. It cost more than $8,000, not counting our own labor, and Daddy sold it 15 years later for $12,000 when he and Momma moved to Dublin to be closer to his work at the Radford arsenal—and, importantly, so Sister could stay at home while attending Radford College.

The house was straight across the road from Ed "Jitney" Funk and his wife, Bell Hill Funk, my mother's aunt. Bell, who for reasons Momma knew but best not discussed here, had married Ed Funk later in life. Ed had children by a previous marriage but none lived with them. Great Aunt Bell—we pronounced it "ant"— had no surviving children of her own, and so seemed to be mostly neutral in the neighborhood squabbles.

Just across the side road to the West was Vernard Carico, whose wife Inez was related to Ed Funk. On down the road a little ways from us and the Funk's was Virgie Akers, whose husband Will worked third shift in the cotton mill all his natural life and, as was usual for the third shifters, looked anemic most of the time. The third shift was looked down on because a worker started there and worked his way to the second and then to the first shift. Will never seemed to be able to work his way off the third shift, so he slept the best he could during the day with his night being fortified with Bromo-Seltzer—and if he was like many others who worked the graveyard shift in the cotton mill, who knows what else was called in for fortification.

Ed Funk, known widely as Jitney, not noted for his special interest in more traditional work, was the community's one and only jitney driver. Jitney was reputed to be a Scots-Irish (or Hilltown) word for cab or taxi—a ride for hire. Jitney Funk made most of his money taking workers, including Bell, the mile or so to the cotton mill at Fries in the mornings and bringing them home in the afternoon. On occasions, he drove folks as far as Galax, 13 miles away, to catch the Greyhound bus or to visit the Kroger store.

After Ed and Bell were married in the 1920s (I was told) when she was in her thirties, more or less, she took, like her brothers, her inheritance from her parents John R. and Martha Jane Corvin Hill, claiming a small share of the several hundred acres they had bought in 1869 and afterward. With family help, Bell and Jitney built a nice five-room house with a smoke house, an outhouse and a chicken house about 300 feet back from the western end of the Hilltown road. Ed parked his jitney in a garage he had built next to the road even though he could open a gate and drive right up to the house.

When Daddy bought his 10 acres and started building the house, Jitney complained to everyone who would listen that his "crow's view" was being blocked. It was true that his view all the way to wild New River Junction was obstructed to a degree by the various structures of our new home place. Most of the men gathered by one of the Jot 'em Down stores in the evenings smiled when they talked about Jitney losing his crow's view because he was well known for just sitting on his front porch and whiling the time away while Bell earned their living on the second shift in the cotton mill.

Virgie Akers, her husband Will and their eight kids leased a house just down the road from everybody. The Akers family was best noted for living on the verge of welfare much of the time and for the rowdiness of some of their kids. Many of the Hilltown area boys had trouble with the Akers.

The Barrett brothers, who sold the *Grit* for a quarter each week, would bicycle out Hilltown Road from U.S. Route 94 at Hawkstown delivering papers to almost every house. The *Grit* was the first truly national newspaper in America and at its height it had more than one million subscribers. One could get it in the mail or boys such as the industrious Barretts would deliver it. The *Grit* was something of a *USA Today*-type newspaper that was and is very family oriented.

The Akers boys would hide in their woodshed (a lean-to on Uncle Jitney's garage) and run out just as the Barretts rode by, knocking them off their bikes. This usually resulted in a rough and tumble, if not bloody, brawl.

The confrontations ended when everyone on our end of the

paper route decided to subscribe to the *Grit* by mail and the Barretts stopped delivering. In a way, the Akers boys had won.

But they had learned well their tactics from attacking the Barrett boys and they used them on me, among others. When going west out on Hilltown Road toward Hawkstown, I always expected an ambush at Ed Funk's garage and it frequently happened. It became a regular topic of conversation around our dinner table with Momma finally getting fed up over her boy being harassed.

On that fateful day, I was returning home at dusk from visiting my cousin Aubrey Hill, whose father had moved them back home and rented a house close to Hawkstown, just about a quarter-mile west of us on the same road. It was getting dark as I rode

Sister Mickey and Daddy at the new Hilltown house about 1950.

my new bicycle home on the dirt and gravel Hilltown Road. Since it was already past dinner time, I knew Momma would have something to say about where I had been and why I was late—and that was something to avoid at all costs. It's no wonder I was hurrying.

Pedaling up the little incline coming past Virgie Akers' house (it was Virgie's and Will's but everyone knew it was Virgie's place), I glanced over my left shoulder to see if there were any of those Akers boys around. Seeing none, I gave a sigh of relief and picked up the pace.

But as I passed ol' Jitney's garage on the edge of the dirt road, the door to the woodshed broke open with a loud *bang*. Out rushed three Akers boys in bib overalls yelling "Knock 'im off, grab the bike! Stop 'im! Git 'im!"

Before I knew what happened, they were all around me and I was on the ground with my shirt torn and my elbows bloody being pelted with rocks and clods of dirt. It was all too obvious to a down and confused 11-year-old that they were angry about something.

As I struggled to my feet, pushing away the smaller Akers boys, I saw my new red and white three-speed bike being rushed back into the woodshed by Billy Akers and the door closing. Once the door was locked from the inside the boys still outside backed off and started poking fun at me. They had my fancy bike and no way could I get it back. I was panicked. I couldn't lose my new bike. What if they tore it up? What would Daddy say?

The commotion had begun to draw a crowd. Jitney and Bell Funk had come out on their front porch to see what was going on. Members of the William Carico family came up their long driveway/dirt road to watch and Will Akers came out on his front porch, such as it was, and leaned against the wall mumbling something with a cigarette hanging out the side of his mouth. Next door Inez and her family looked from the porch and out the side window to see what was going on. Later I learned that Harl Williams our neighbor who lived just at the top of the hill to the other direction watched and drew his own opinions. Everybody in the neighborhood was a witness of sorts to this event or so it seemedh.

And the standoff—me fighting off the smaller boys and beating on the woodshed door with rocks and large sticks from the gully at the edge of the road—was just that, a commotion-filled standoff.

Then one of the little Akers boys was hit in the head with a rock, either by me or one of his brothers, and that brought his big Momma out her back door up the main road, coming to straighten me out. She looked large and menacing as she strode directly at me though, I now know she was about five feet two inches tall—but almost as wide as she was tall.

I couldn't deal with her but I couldn't back off either for they had my new bike in their woodshed. It was getting scary. What would she do? What could I do?

Then my little sister came to the rescue. At the first sign of trouble she had run home and told Momma. Just as things were getting bad, there came Momma striding forward to do battle. She was angry and fed up with this kinda' stuff. Both women arrived about the same time. My momma was daunting, which gave me considerable relief. At 36 years of age and five foot seven she was still the second tallest person in all Hilltown. And since my sister had arrived in 1945 she was no longer the slender shapely woman so clearly etched in my memory. She had begun to enjoy the fruits of middle age and now was a full-figured woman who was later referred to by Will in court as a "battle-axe."

It was clear that she was coming to do battle for she was good and tired of the endless sniping and harassing we had endured from the Akers' since we had moved to west Hilltown in the summer of 1948 when Daddy finished our new house. This was the showdown she had almost seemed to be waiting for. In a powerful voice that caught everybody by surprise Momma yelled, "Git away from my boy! I said git and I mean git!" She stood, if possible, even taller. "Git that bike out here to Wade or I'm going to call the sheriff and have somebody arrested!" She thought about it for a moment, and then said, "I may call him anyway!"

That hit a raw nerve in Virgie, as members of her family frequently had brushes with the law, particularly the sheriff's departments in Carroll and Grayson counties. She almost exploded, blaming me for everything.

"It's that son-of-a-bitch's fault, he started it," she yelled at Momma, pointing her finger at me. "He started it running his fancy bike at my boys trying to run 'em down! We're going to fix him! We're taking that bike! We got 'hit!"

Momma, unfazed by the commentary on my lineage, was focused on getting me and the bike back in our yard as soon as possible. Daddy was coming home, and even though he in his size and countenance could quickly bring things to an end, this was Momma's fight and she wanted it ended right now. She walked over to the woodshed door and jerked it wide open, exposing Billy Akers standing there with the bike. He was stunned.

Momma said, "Wade, come over here and git this bike. Take it to the basement."

Virgie was infuriated. She picked up a pole and waved it at me. "I'll take care of you, you bastard."

That did it.

Momma might not react to someone calling her son a son-of-a-bitch but I was no bastard and she wasn't about to let anyone get by with calling me one. She had waited until she was almost 24 years old to marry and I wasn't born until 10 months later. Hilltown had its share of admitted and non-admitted bastards but I wasn't one and she wasn't going to let Virgie get away with calling me one. No, buddy!

As I pushed the bike toward our yard Momma turned to Virgie and said, "What did you call my boy?"

"He's a son-of-a-bitch, *a bastard*," Virgie yelled.

Momma yelled back, "He's no *bastard*." With a stick in her hand she advanced toward Virgie, who reconsidered and moved backwards toward her hard red clay yard one step at a time. Now she, not Momma, was declaring, "I'm calling the sheriff! I'm calling the sheriff! You just wait!"

"You do that, you bitch," Momma yelled. Now that was different. I had never heard Momma use cuss words before—and hardly ever afterwards. "I'm going to give you a whipping your Momma ought to have given you a long time ago! And your lard ass, lazy cousins can't help you now," she raged.

The Akers retreated back down the road, a quarter of a mile or so, into their house and we went home to put the bike away, finish supper and wait for Daddy, who was working at Steven's Creek building a house for some people. Sister was quiet—which was unusual.

Normally in Hilltown, such events would end right there and then with everybody claiming a victory of sorts. But that was not Virgie's way as she enjoyed combat and, while shying away from a personal physical account, she wanted revenge and she would have her day in court. Literally.

Though it seemed over for a while, the sheriff showed up five days later with a summons for Momma to appear in Carroll County Court in Hillsville to answer charges that she had physically threatened Virgie and her boys and had 'cussed in public. That was how Momma went to court for the first and only time in her life.

Daddy arranged for an attorney, a man named Rollie Cottrill who was something of an apprentice of Judge Mathews. Mr. Cottrill was one of the lawyers who hung out around the courthouse and would be there anyway.

We left early the morning of the big trial—all of us, including my small sister. Arriving early, we conferred with lawyer Cottrill for a few minutes and then went in to wait as Judge Mathews worked steadily and methodically through a long list of cases ranging from theft to marital problems to disputes among neighbors. The latter category certainly included us and the Akers.

When our case was called, the prosecutor read the charges and Judge Mathews called on Virgie to tell her side of the story. Then he called Momma to give her version. Momma told it just as it happened, including the cuss words she used on Virgie. After the two of them finished, the judge asked if there was anyone else who wanted to testify. There being none, he immediately rendered his decision. He seemed to know exactly what he was doing, like he had been through this before.

The Judge said he understood how Momma was frustrated and

how she had a right to be—but she just could not threaten people in that way. It was unlawful. He didn't want to see any of them back there again. And he didn't like that language that both women used.

In the end he announced Momma's fine, which brought Virgie to her feet in protest. She was really upset. All this trouble and the judge was fining Momma just five dollars that was outrageous according to Virgie. The judge turned to her and laid it on the line. She had to make her boys behave better and that the next time she came to court with a case like this he was not going to stand for it. It was a waste of county time and money. Unbeknownst to us, Virgie had been there before and had an inclination to take people by warrant. She had done the same thing to the Barrett family before they gave up the *Grit* route.

Momma paid the fine and declared, "It was the best damn five dollars I ever spent in my life."

One could certainly not argue about the satisfaction it had bought her. Not only had Momma told off Virgie that evening, but she got to go to the Carroll County Courthouse and tell the world about Virgie and her family. She had had her say and things were going to be different. Judge Mathews had said so.

She felt good standing in the parking lot outside the courthouse that bright colorful autumn day and it showed.

The rest of us felt good, too. Sister was happy and Daddy wore a funny half baked smile for the rest of the day. It was the best "damn" five dollars "we" had ever spent!

Hobnobbing with the Splendid Splinter

"Come on, sit here with me," the big guy in a Red Sox baseball uniform said patting the seat beside him in the dugout. "Where are you from, boy? Bluefield?"

For a minute I was stunned!

Then I scrambled over the fence into the dugout and plopped down on the bench beside him.

He looked different from his pictures. Sitting there in the dirt floor dugout under the shingled roof wearing a rumpled, road weary uniform, Ted Williams looked thin compared to his newspaper pictures, more human and less heroic. But this was the guy who hit .400 in a season, volunteered for WW II and interrupted his baseball career again to fly 39 missions for the marines in Korea. He was a national hero. He was Ted Williams. And I was sitting beside him!

For an eighth grade baseball freak it was like getting high on a beer—not that I ever did—I could hardly believe my good fortune. I actually got to sit beside Ted Williams in the dugout while Jimmy Piersall, Eddie Mathews and Warren Spahn warmed up on the field for a preseason Red Sox and Braves game.

It was seventh heaven!

But the next day, I learned that the occasional touch of heaven wasn't without its consequences—in the form of Principal Ned.

"Was it worth it?" He ran a hand through his gray-shot crew cut and frowned at me from across his wide, imposing desk. "Was it worth losing an eight year record of perfect attendance? Was it worth losing your straight A average? Was one baseball game worth all that?" He paused and I cringed, knowing what was coming next. He dropped his voice and intoned, "What is your Momma going to say?"

I had no reply. We cherished that perfect attendance record, and the As too. Momma was not going to be happy. Then Principal Ned lowered the boom for good. "I'm going to have to suspend you for the rest of the week. All the other boys need to know this sort of thing will not be tolerated."

My heart stopped. I felt sick to my stomach. He was suspending me for four days, all because I'd hooked *once*? What was Momma going to say? I shook my head. There was no use arguing with Principal Ned. Those who tried had lived to regret it.

As I walked out of the office, I saw Mitch, my best friend, waiting for his visit with the principal. He had caused the problem in the first place—that crazy Red Sox fan. When he found out that the Red Sox and the Boston Braves were playing an exhibition baseball game in Bluefield, Virginia he went on a mission to maneuver a way to go see them play. He'd talked his daddy into taking a car load of us to see the game.

Now Mitch waited for his turn in the hot seat. (He should have been first.) His head seemed to be on a swivel as he attempted to look at me and keep an eye on the principal's office at the same time.

"Wwwhat happened?" he stuttered. Mitch only stuttered when he was good and nervous.

"I'll tell you what," I said, glaring at my erstwhile best friend. "He suspended me for the rest of the week for skipping class yesterday. And it's your fault."

"Mmmy fault," he stuttered, "How is that? What did I do?"

"You thought up the whole thing. You talked your daddy into taking us. You got me into trouble." I crossed my arms and glared harder, ignoring the fact that it had—sort of—been my idea in the first place.

"Suspend you? What is he going to do with me? How about me?" Mitch whispered, not wanting to attract the attention of the office secretary. He hoped Mr. Ned might just forget about him.

"You'll get suspended but that's a lot easier than what I got," I replied. "I have to go home and tell Momma that I'm suspended, lost my perfect attendance record and my straight A average." I shook my head, already picturing the look of disappointment that was going to be plastered across Momma's face. "You won't have to go confess because your daddy took us. He knows already what you did. Momma doesn't know. I have to tell her everything."

I blasted Mitch with both barrels, not because I was all that mad at him, but because I dreaded facing Momma. I thought I had gotten away with that wonderful, perfect day at the ballpark.

"What about Swanny?" Mitch said. "Does Mr. Ned know he went, too?"

"Heck! Swanny is better off than we are. He got his big brother to bring in a note yesterday asking to be excused. He's gettin' off Scot free. He's smarter than the two of us put together."

I shook my head again and went home to face Momma.

I would've rather sat in with Mr. Ned for another hour.

"Son, was it worth it?" Momma asked when I'd confessed.

"We saw the Braves and the Red Sox play and Ted Williams spoke to me and Mitch," I answered lamely, looking down at the kitchen table for inspiration.

"I said, was it worth eight years of perfect attendance and your straight A average?" she responded. Momma seemed plenty calm but I couldn't take that intense burning in her eyes. I couldn't look her straight in the face.

I hung my head thinking of how I had gotten into this trouble. It was partly my fault. Well, more than partly. I had read in the newspapers that the Red Sox and my Boston Braves were playing their way north to Boston after spring training in Florida. They were to play in towns and small cities where one or the other had a farm club—Statesboro, Mt. Airy and then Bluefield. Mitch and everybody else I knew was either a Red Sox or a Yankees fan so I had to be different. Thus, I had adopted the Braves and found they were more interesting anyway.

Bluefield! Why, that was just across the mountains about sixty miles away. I had been there several times with my Daddy and Uncle G'Burn as they hauled coal from West Virginia to the textile towns of North Carolina. I wanted to go to Bluefield and see that game! I called Mitch and he went wild about the possibility of seeing the Red Sox play. He was the biggest Red Sox fan ever. Before long Mitch had the trip all worked out. His daddy would take us and his brother C and maybe Swanny, too.

The game was on Monday—a school day and I had not missed school for any reason including bad colds and funerals for seven years. But this would be my first and maybe my only chance to see the Braves play baseball, 'cause we lived deep in the Appalachian Mountains and famous people didn't come our way that often. No use telling Momma, much less asking her permission, because she thought everything began and ended with school.

Ergo, I wouldn't tell her. What she didn't know wouldn't hurt her, right?

Everything was planned. I got up early Monday morning and hustled to milk the cow, eat my breakfast, change clothes and prepare to leave. I didn't want questions. I waited until Momma was in the basement before I hurried out and headed toward

Hawkstown instead of towards Fries, where I went to school. Soon, I reached old Route 94 and there were the Mitchells waiting in their brand new 1951 Ford four-door sedan. Mitch's dad glanced over his shoulder at me and said, pointedly, "How's your daddy?" I just said okay and he let it drop. This excursion was between me and Momma.

As we started out ol' 94 past the Pickett's house, Mitch turned and looked over his shoulder at me, "Wish we'd asked ol' Ken if he wanted to go?" He was talking about our buddy Kenneth Lanter who had showed us the first tape recorder we had ever seen and later inspired Mitch to buy a guitar and enter the country music business. I responded, "Me too. Why didn't you?"

The trip north to Bluefield on the Virginia-West Virginia line was uneventful although we crossed three mountains with more than twenty hairpin curves on an old two lane road. Once we got there, we enjoyed a rack of hotdogs and French fries before going to the Virginia side of town for the game. This was our big day!

We wandered around the ballpark, checking off who was there, who was warming up and what Piersall was saying. It was well known that Jimmy Piersall was not only a great ball player but a talker as well. (Piersall was also well known for his fight with mental illness the discussion of which was pretty much taboo in those days. His book, *Fear Strikes Out,* was the subject of a movie starring Anthony Perkins in the 1950s.)

Mitch was anxiously looking for Ted Williams, his idol. In fact, Ted Williams was everyone's idol. He seemed so perfect. Not only was he a great hitter, but he was modest in his stardom. One year when he had something of a slump for him, Williams asked the Red Sox management for a reduction in salary. (Quite a contrast to today.) Even a Boston Braves fan like me had to admire the great Ted Williams.

We looked and looked, but we couldn't spot him.

Where was the Splendid Splinter?

Soon we heard Piersall's voice coming from the dugout. Jimmy was insisting that someone pick up a ball that had rolled dead in front of the dugout and throw it back out to him just beyond the first base. This event captured our attention. We saw a tall lean man in a Red Sox uniform walk a couple of steps out of the dugout, look into right field, bend over, pick up the ball and throw it to Jimmy.

When the player turned and gave Piersall an 'aw shucks go on your way' wave, we recognized him as the person we were looking for—the great Ted Williams. Just as he ducked to enter the dugout he glanced over.

And looked straight at us and smiled.

This was the inspiration we needed. Mitch ran to the other end of the dugout and leaned over and as quick as you could say Jack Frost he slipped one leg over and disappeared into the dugout.

Emboldened by Mitch's success I hustled down to this dugout even though I was going to root for the Braves. Leaning over the fence I saw Ted "Theodore" Williams signing a baseball. Mitch grabbed the ball and bounced back across the fence to show his dad and C what he had—a baseball autographed by Ted Williams, his idol.

I was still leaning over the fence when Williams looked up and said, "Come on over here, boy."

In a split second I was there sitting on the bench beside the Splendid Splinter himself.

Williams looked at me, wearing his baseball hat cocked to one side and said, "Where are you boys from?"

"Fries. Fries, Virginia," I retorted knowing full well that no one from Boston would know of the place. Not a star like Williams.

"Ever see ol' Coaker Triplett play ball over there?" Williams replied.

Oh, My God! I thought. *He knows where Fries is because he knows that Coaker Triplett plays in the Virginia-Carolina (industrial) League and the Fries cotton mill had a team in that league.*

"I've known Coaker since he played for the Cardinals in '39, '40 and '41 before Musial beat him out," Williams continued. "You ever meet him?"

I tried not to babble. "No, well uh no. But I've seen him play. One night he hit three homers with two going over the lights and out of the ballpark down in Fries."

"He sure could hit," Williams agreed. He looked down at me and asked, "Do you have a ball for me to sign?" When I shook my head 'no', he smiled and handed me an unsigned ball, saying, "As a big Braves fan you don't have to tell anyone who gave this to you." He grinned at my logo sweatshirt and winked.

I pocketed the ball, jumped back over the fence into the stands and watched the game, which the Braves won. And I was content listening to Mitch explain (again and again) just why the Red Sox lost as we drove back home. All the while I could feel this special baseball in my pocket.

Years later, after I had graduated from engineering school, Momma asked me again. "Was it worth it? Was it worth losing your perfect attendance record?"

And I finally had an answer. "Yes, Momma," I said, "It was really worth it. But if I could do it again, I'd get that baseball signed."

After Hobnobbing—The New River.

"You wait!" Momma said abruptly cutting off all conversation about my trip to Bluefield to see the Braves and Ted Williams. "You just wait 'til your daddy hears about this! He's not going to be happy about you losing your perfect attendance for one old ballgame. You wait."

That was all she had to say before heading out to catch her ride to the Fries cotton mill. It was going to be a long evening, but it was Tuesday and Daddy would be home. I milked the cows early, took our supper out of the warming oven so we could eat, helped my sister get settled and waited... and waited.

When Daddy finally showed up about 8 o'clock I met him at the door and confessed all before he hardly got in the door.

He listened patiently before saying anything. Then he said, "Well first, who won the game the Braves or those old Red Sox?"

Encouraged by this beginning I blurted out, "The Braves won and I met Ted Williams. He is as tall as you and a lot skinnier." I wished I hadn't added that thing about being skinny 'cause Daddy was always worrying about his weight.

He continued, "Tell me where you guys had lunch. Wasn't at Louie's Dog and Burger was it?" Back in his railroad days he had spent time in the N&W operations there and had enjoyed the town's many places to eat.

Finally after much preliminary talk about the day he got around to the meat of the thing, "I know all about it. Mr. Ned called your Momma and she knew it all when you came home. She called me and we've decided you'll have to stay at home for the rest of the week and study your school lessons. No playing baseball or biking up and down Hilltown Road. Just stay home."

Today kids call that being grounded.

As he ate supper, my mind raced a thousand miles a minute thinking of the possibilities and I just blurted it out, "After I get my school work and other jobs done could I walk over in Leff Carico's fields? Over toward the river?"

He leaned his tall frame back in the white kitchen chair. "I think you could. But you'll have to do all the chores your momma gives you before she leaves for the mill at 2:30."

The first day of suspension was tough because Momma didn't work on Wednesdays (the mill was on a four day work week) and she had lots for me to do. On the second day, I worked around the house milking, doing my homework, helping Momma here and there and eating lunch with her. As soon as she left for the mill I hustled out the back door and scampered through the hilly pastureland on through Leff Carico's fields toward the river.

The New River not only led to the founding of Fries in 1901 via the creation of the dam for the production of electricity; but had for generations helped define the life and culture of Hilltown. When John R. and Martha Jane Hill settled there in 1869 they owned several hundred acres of rolling, hilly farmland defined in part by a long, two-mile stretch of the ancient river flowing north toward the great Ohio.

Although it was no longer the major economic factor it had once been, we were constantly aware of its presence. It was a beautiful stream cutting through the mountains directly behind and about a half-mile from our house, always an attraction for boys and men alike. It offered beauty and solace and fresh air and free flowing water. The famous Double Shoals were within easy walking distance of our house.

By following an old dirt road I soon found myself on a ridge covered by large white pine trees overlooking the rolling whitewaters of the Double Shoals, formed as the river cut thorough a mountain more than a million years ago. I could see downriver, between steep, forested mountainsides, and there was a train coming up the tracks puffing white smoke as regularly as a clock ticking.

It was the afternoon N&W train with a steam engine pulling one passenger car, three freight cars, a flatbed, and a caboose. This train, called the New River Express, ran from Pulaski to Fries each morning, then backed down the river to Fries Junction, on up Chestnut Creek to Galax. After unloading and loading in Galax, the train backed down to the Junction and then up to Fries before heading for Pulaski about 4 o'clock in the afternoon. It never turned, but moved forward and backward and forward and finally back down the 21 miles down to Pulaski.

This afternoon it had finished its trip to Galax and was on its way to complete a second pass through Fries. The train schedule demonstrated the importance of the cotton mill as an industrial center. While Galax was larger than Fries, its focus was on furniture. Materials and finished products were trucked to and from North Carolina. So Fries got two trains a day while bigger Galax got one.

As I lay on the hillside with my hands behind my neck watching the chugging train I spotted two boys not much bigger than me standing on a rock fishing the whitewaters of the rapids. It was Ne-nee and Dirty, two of my cousins. Both had dropped out of school after finishing the seventh and eight grades, respectively. *So this was what they do while I suffer through six periods each day under the watchful eyes of my teachers*, I thought with more than a touch of envy.

I tumbled down the mountainside and arrived at the tracks just after old Number 36 had passed. I hurried to a path leading down to the river close to where Ne-nee and Dirty were fishing. They had a flat-bottomed boat tied to the big rock they were fishing from so I hollered, "Hey guys. Could y'all come and get me?"

Dirty, looked for a minute and yelled something back. It was then I realized that I couldn't hear over the rushing and foaming white water. They couldn't hear me either. I kept calling, "Come and get me! Come and get me!"

Finally, Dirty seemed to grasp what I was asking, but waved me off disdainfully. He wasn't about to go to that much trouble for an underage schoolboy cousin. Ne-nee kept on fishing. He didn't even look my way.

Dirty yelled something and moved his arms in a swimming motion.

Swim over? I thought to myself. That was something I hadn't considered. I could swim after a fashion having taken some lessons at the YMCA pool the summer before, but swimming through that swirling, churning whitewater was another thing.

Concluding that neither Dirty nor Ne-nee was going to help, I sat down, took off my shoes and socks, rolled up my britchey legs and pulled off my sweatshirt, leaving only a cotton undershirt covering my chest.

Still, I thought it over several minutes. *Am I gonna get into trouble? What if the water is too fast?* Finally, ignoring my second thoughts, I jumped in and started toward the rock. At first I could walk on the bottom. As I drew nearer the rock the water became deeper and swifter and I started swimming toward the upper end of the 20- by 15-foot boulder. The river pulled me downstream. When they saw me struggling, both Dirty and Ne-nee caught hold of me and pulled me up on the huge gray rock with them.

I was wet and chilled by the wind. But it was glorious standing in the middle of Double Shoals with the wild mountain river rushing by toward Buck Dam more than a mile away.

We spent the rest of the afternoon on the big rock until shadows grew long and Dirty declared it was time to go. He untied the boat and let me and Ne-nee get in before he jumped in himself. Grabbing one of the poles—no paddles, just long poles to push and guide the boat with—we started inching toward shore.

Rounding the front of the rock the swift current caught our boat and spun it for a minute. Dirty and Ne-nee used their poles to regain control as I held on for dear life. But the quick violent movements of the boat every which way toppled me out and under the roiling waters.

To my surprise Dirty jumped in the foaming river after me. Ne-nee struggled with the boat as it drifted not to the shore but down the middle of the angry stream. Dirty and I went rushing past the boat with his hand tightly grasping my T-shirt. The rushing and gushing stream turned us around and around with one us seemingly under the water at any one time.

"Help us. Help us!" we both yelled at the top of our voices but we didn't know if he heard or not. We clung together for dear life as Ne-nee and the boat caught up in swift but less turbulent water. He finally was able to stabilize the boat, lay the poles in the bottom and lean over the side to pull both of us in.

We got to shore completely soaked and exhausted. *I've never been in that kind of trouble before,* I thought to myself, not willing to appear worried. After resting, we waded upstream toward my clothing, dragging the boat with us. We had drifted almost a half mile and it was not easy struggling upstream with that boat. Finally, laying on the bank regaining some composure, we began to make light of the incident.

"It was really a lot of fun. We'll do it again!" Ne-nee declared bravely.

The shadows of spring grew long as we walked home up the hollers to Hilltown Road, tired and dragging. We each turned to go toward our respective homes as darkness fell. Dirty asked, "Hey, what are you guys doing tomorrow?"

Doing? Well I was suspended from school and had one more day of punishment but they didn't know that.

"I'm going to the river," I boldly said, "how about you?"

They, being completely free, seemed to like the idea. Always the leader, Dirty declared, "Well, I tell you what. We'll meet at the boat about one in the afternoon and do some fishing. What do you say to that?"

So, the next day was another great New River adventure—we

actually caught some fish and watched the train go by twice. And none of us fell in the water. The week that began with a great baseball adventure in Bluefield ended with a wild, wonderful river adventure.

My grades did get lowered a letter. And my perfect attendance record was gone forever. But I discovered a new world. The world of a wild river was one I would rediscover many times in the years to follow.

And I could answer Momma... in another context "Yes, Momma it was really worth it!"

Juvenile Delinquent, Almost

"What are you going to tell your daddy about this?" Momma said as she walked into the living room where I was sitting by the Warm Morning heating stove. She was waving a piece of paper in her hand, shaking it at me. "You know the sheriff wanted to arrest you. He wanted to take you to Hillsville to jail, don't you know?" she asked that Monday in 1951.

The deputy sheriff had just left and she had the warrant in her hand. While it was technically a warrant for arrest, it was in reality a summons to Carroll County Court on the third Monday in February to answer charges that I and others had rocked Jimmy Rife's house the previous Thursday night. It was a summons not just for me and several other boys (mostly cousins) of Hilltown, but a summons for Momma and Daddy to bring me to court. That was what she had agreed to and what had sent the deputy on his way back across the New River to Hillsville and the Carroll County Court House.

Oh, I remembered the night in vivid detail, and had hoped I would never have to explain things to Momma or Daddy. I knew they would be upset. I had gotten into this mess without trying.

The words of a cousin had started everything, and they were etched into my mind. "Who's going down the holler with me to set that Jimmy Rife straight? He's gotta' understand that he don't mess with us."

The provocative statement had been thrown out by my older first cousin, once removed, Frank (Snotty) Hill, standing in the middle of the Horace "G'burn" Hill's Jot 'em Down country store in Hilltown that cold January evening in 1952.

"We will. Yeah, let's go. Let's show him, he can't mess with us," the angry group (mostly cousins) responded.

"We'll get him!"

I had just walked into the store out of the cold night air on my way home from the Fries High School eighth grade basketball team's practice at the YMCA that evening. I still had to milk our cow, eat some supper and then maybe read some of my school assignments for the next day. But nonetheless, I'd stopped in the Jot 'em Down store for a break—and to see what was going on.

I stood just inside the front door with my blue cotton toboggan on my head (covering the first crew cut in Fries that barber Charlie Anders had crafted from a magazine article I had taken in), my red wool Mackinaw pulled up around my ears and my high topped Converse sneakers tied around my neck by the laces. I was taken aback by the boys' excitement and anger.

There were eight or ten of them, from 14 to 17 years old, milling around the glowing red pot bellied coal stove angrily talking about what that Jimmy Rife had done and how "we" would make him pay for it.

"We'll show him!"

The group was ready to go down the narrow dirt path leading from the Hilltown Road to the Sutphin Brothers' place to confront Rife. Jimmy, 19 years old, his 17-year-old wife and their year-old baby lived in a two-room shack about 300 feet off the main road. The shack was in pretty bad shape, having no indoor plumbing and seemingly not painted for decades. Neither had gotten past the third grade and they were one of the few families in our area who would take welfare if they could get it. Looking back, they were in a bad state or so it seemed, and our Hilltown mothers worried about the health of the baby. It was always "the baby."   The complaint against Jimmy Rife was that he had destroyed the piney woods lean-to just up the hillside from the shack he lived in. Some of the other guys had built the lean-to as a hangout where they could smoke and chew tobacco, among other things, during their long, idle hours each day. Most had long since dropped out of school, but in some cases their parents had yet to discover that fact.

The lean-to was built out of pine boughs and had a thick pine needle floor for lounging and sleeping. They were proud of it.

But when he and some of the other boys had stopped by on that cold, snowy January day to check on the lean-to, they had found it demolished and the parts strewn over the forest floor. On their way up to the Hilltown road they had seen Rife and wife and had asked if they knew anything about the lean-to, only to be cussed out. This was standard behavior for Jimmy, but his attitude led the boys to conclude that he had done the deed.

And now Jimmy was going to pay one way or the other if Snotty and cousins had their way—and could get the whole gang to go down there.

As the group was obviously going down the holler to confront Rife, I was in a quandary. I needed to go on home to my chores and supper, but the guys expected me to go with them and I couldn't say no. Could I?

I craved their acceptance but they saw me only as a bookworm. As the only one who would ever graduate from high school, I wasn't exactly popular with them. I knew if I was to win the respect of those older cousins I would have to be part of the gang taking its revenge on Jimmy Rife. I would go with them!

It was an exciting moment, a moment of drama and suspense in addition to one of uncontrolled excitement. We ran out of the store, heading back down the path to Fries that I had just taken minutes earlier. That night I would retrace my steps twice—to my ultimate chagrin.

It was getting colder and darker as we trudged down the road. Snotty broke into a half trot and the rest of us followed single file down the small dirt path past Grandpa Hill's spring house and down to the old house. We were going to confront that Jimmy Rife! He couldn't get away with tearing down our lean-to!

Then we were there! The house was completely dark. He couldn't afford electricity and had only kerosene lamps, which were apparently out. I moved on past the group to be on the Fries side of the shack, eager to see every thing that was going on. The weather beaten shack was a two-room affair, one room serving as the kitchen and living area and the other the bedroom area. Having once been inside, I knew it had a wood burning cooking stove and a small but seldom used Warm Morning heater in the living room.

It was probably less than 600 square feet of living space not counting the open air basement used for storage. The well was up the hill on the south side of the house and the outdoor toilet was on the western downhill side. Someone obviously had known what they were doing in designing the facilities. The house had several windows, some of which were covered only with cloth.

Tonight it was seemed the Rife's knew we were coming. The house was totally dark.

Someone yelled, "Jimmy Rife, Jimmy Rife, come out here and answer some questions!"

Silence. Rife was laying low.

He yelled again, "Jimmy Rife, where are you?"

There was a muffled answer, "We're in bed. Get outta here! God Dammit!"

That infuriated some of the Hilltown boys. Several started yelling and then, suddenly, there it was. Crash! A rock hit the side of the house. Even to this day no one admits knowing who threw that first rock but it ignited an intense bombardment by almost everyone there. Some of the missiles crashed through cloth window coverings, one smashed through glass. Finally a light came on and the door was thrown open. Standing there for all to see was a furious Jimmy. "Come out you cowards! Hurting my woman and my baby, I'll see you in hell!"

Suddenly our gang wasn't a gang any more—just a bunch of frightened kids fleeing Jimmy's wrath helter skelter. I ran down the holler to Church Street in Fries and back to the YMCA where I went in with a couple of the others. I hung around the "Y" for a while, wondering how I was ever going to get back up the mountain to our house and milk those cows. I was past worrying about supper or school tomorrow. How would I get home and get things in order before Momma found out and how could I stay low so that no one would know I was one of the vigilantes?

I heard a commotion outside the Y. Without thinking, I rushed outside to see what was happening. There stood Jimmy Rife in the middle of the street arguing with one of my cousins.

He was livid. "Somebody's gonna' pay for that window!" he declared.

I blurted out, "What's going on here?"

Jimmy recognized me, "That you, Wade Gilley? What are you doing' here? You part of this?"

I was stunned. Jimmy had come point blank to the awful truth. I had been part of the attack even though I had not thrown a single rock. Still, I had yelled a few times.

Jimmy turned back to the other guy and began arguing again. I was worried but relieved. He'd never blame me. And with that thought I hustled home, milked the cow and took my supper out of the oven where Momma had left it and ate. Then I went to bed without turning the television on. I was still anxious,

The next day was Friday and I went to school at Fries but came home early after the eighth grade homeroom teacher noticed that I had a yellow look about me. It turned out that I had the yellow jaundice and was confined home for almost a week.

That next Monday, I sat by the Warm Morning heater in the living room reading and suffering through a day at home while my mother cleaned the house and got herself ready to go into the cotton mill for the second shift—3-11 p.m. She had kept me home and made sure I was wrapped up and sitting by the heater.

A car pulled up out front. It was a government type vehicle, brown or dark green with no markings. But it was a government car for sure.

A man got out and donned his wide brimmed hat, pulling it close to his ears. It was a sheriff or deputy sheriff. We Hilltown boys could recognize a sheriff from any distance. This was one.

He opened the gate to our white picket fence and came up the walk to the house. He knocked on the door as I listened and wondered, dread creeping slowly over me.

Momma went to the door and talked to him for a minute and

then followed him outside, stood in the cold and had a more extensive conversation. Then she came back in and came to the living room staring a hole through me. She shook the paper in her hand directly at me declaring, "Wade, you've gone and done it now. Wait 'til your daddy hears about this. You're in real trouble!"

She was right. Jimmy had taken me and Snotty and another guy by warrant. He charged us with rocking his house and endangering his wife and baby. We had to appear in circuit court in Hillsville before Judge Mathews in two weeks. This was serious. Judge Mathews was known for being hard. A red haired, no nonsense lawyer, he served part time as judge while hoping for elevation to the full time bench and a state retirement, Daddy explained to me that night. Judge Mathews was no one to fool with.

It didn't sound good at all. We were in trouble I could tell from Daddy's voice and grim look.

"What can we do?" I asked.

"We'll just tell the truth and Judge Mathews will do the right thing," he said. I wasn't so sure but Daddy was still the all-knowing authority figure in our family. After all, he was six foot five and a security guard at the Radford Arsenal by this time. He was a law and order type guy.

On returning to school I got the word—second hand because I was the only one still going to school—that Snotty and the other guy were going to plead innocent and they expected me to do the same. I was in a box. The other guys and their families were denying everything, but Daddy had said I was to 'fess up. How could I navigate this quandary? Besides, I didn't actually see anybody throw anything but I was there when the rocks were thrown. I could confess to that.

The next week was really nerve wracking. Even though the other defendants were not in school, all my other cousins were and they were knew about the tensions between Snotty and me. And he was older and more experienced.

I wondered every day, "Will they get me on the way to school or on the way home?" I made sure that I found someone to walk to school with. Usually that meant cousin Wanda Sue Hill, who was two grades ahead of me and a no nonsense person herself.

Wanda's nickname was Gander, given to her by her daddy, P'toke, and her mother, Callie, because she grew fast and seemed lanky to them. But she always handled herself with grace and poise even though as a very young child she had seemed gangly. Gander was also meant nice to look at.

For some reason I felt secure walking down the dirt road through the pine trees with Gander on the way to school. At least if Snotty and the others took out after me there would be a witness.

We had the written court summons in our house forever it seemed. The presence of those two sheets of paper created enormous tension.

Three weeks later on a Monday, we dressed up and drove from Hilltown to Hillsville. To get there we went through Fries, up the New River to Route 58, which traversed the southern part of Virginia from Bristol to Norfolk, covering more than 300 miles. .

Finally, we appeared in Judge Mathews' court and I told the story as it had happened. I shall never forget sitting on that witness stand, the only time I was ever in any court, responding to the questions of the commonwealth's attorney with everyone listening. It was especially tough in the face of the looks I got from Snotty, his family and the others. But in the end he and the other boy 'fessed up, too. (Several who were there got off clean as could be.)

Judge Mathews said, "Well, you boys got into something you shouldn't have and you'll just have to pay. You all will have to pay court costs. Can't expect the people of Carroll County to pay these costs. That should be about $20 apiece, being as how there are three of you."

He leaned over his high bench and did some arithmetic on a piece of paper and said, "Twenty-four dollars and ninety five cents apiece should do it." Then he added, "But you need to know that this is a wrong thing you done over there in that holler. Each of you will have to pay a $15 fine." He continued in his gruff voice, "I hope you boys understand that I don't ever want to see any one of you here again. Do you understand?"

We all shook our heads and said, "Yes, yes sir."

Everyone was anxious to get out of there because we could see that the old judge meant business. It wasn't a time to argue.

Judge Mathews continued, "Now, Mr. Rife has a broken window that will have to be fixed. How are you boys going to take care of that?"

Daddy stood up and said, "Judge Mathews, sir."

"Yes, Woodrow, what do you have to say?"

"Well, I think that me and Earl (Snotty's father and my first cousin once removed) and the boys, we'll get together and take care of that. We can replace the window in just a little bit of time."

Before the Judge could respond Jimmy Rife stood up from his chair beside the Commonwealth's Attorney and said, "Judge Mathews can I speak?"

"Well," the judge said, "I would hope so. What do you have to add?"

"Well, Judge, I've already spent my own money to get the window fixed. Its wintertime and the baby and my wife were cold. It cost me almost $9 to get those panes put back in," Jimmy said.

Judge Mathews leaned back in his chair. "Did you put them panes in yourself?"

"Well, my brother came over and we bought the panes and put them in. Me and my brother, we did it."

Judge Mathews looked at the other guys and me. "Well, I think you boys owe Mr. Rife $5 apiece for replacing the window panes, including the labor he and his brother expended. You can pay him before leaving today."

The cost was going up —$44.95, way more than Momma made in the cotton mill for a week's work spinning the cotton into threads. But it had to be paid because Judge said so. It would be long time before Momma would let me forget this day.

But it was over and we were eager to get out of there.

Then Judge Mathews said, "Well, there is one more thing...."

One more thing? We were paying the fine, the court costs and for fixing the window. What else could there be?

"I'm worried about you boys and I don't want to see you here again. But I don't want to do anything to harm your futures," he said. "I don't want you to have a criminal record, so I'm going to tell you what I'm going to do. You boys will be on probation until you are 18 or graduated from high school or show the court evidence that you have a full time job or join the Army." He continued, "And, I'm going to suspend the fine. If you're back here before I clear your permanent records you'll be fined for this and whatever else you've done. If I don't see you again before that time then I'll completely clear your record. It will be as though you've never done anything wrong."

For the first time in a long time there was good news and it wasn't just about being on limited term probation. Our punishment had been reduced by $15 to $29.95 apiece. Momma would be glad to hear that, even though in the end she didn't take it that way.

She never did admit that she had been saved any money. In Hilltown in 1953 with the Great Depression still strong in memories and in the middle of what my daddy (a lifelong Democrat) called "Ike-anomics" or what we would now call a recession, a dollar was a dollar. And getting the fine set aside was not saving money if one had to pay all those other costs.

Still, it was a relief. Riding back to Hilltown with Daddy, eating a good dinner cooked by Momma and getting a good night's sleep seemed to set the world straight.

The good feeling lasted until the next day. As I walked from our house out the Hilltown road past the Jot 'em Down toward Wanda Sue's house, I saw the two other guys hanging outside the store watching me. Crossing over to the opposite side I hustled by and went straight into Wanda Sue's house and waited in the kitchen with her mother, Callie for her to get ready to go on down the road to school.

The tension remained for months. At Easter time Snotty told everybody that he didn't get some new clothes because Wade had snitched. It seemed that from then on whenever one of those boys didn't have something it was my fault because I had snitched and we had all had to pay the price. I felt their presence and was frequently looking over my shoulder. But in time they got over it and were again good cousins if not friends.

Going back to school was not hard but living things down was.

Growing-Up Pains

The following Saturday when I was getting ready to go to the picture show Daddy said, "Wade, I think I'll go to the show with you tonight."

Go with me? This was something new and would really cramp my style. What would everyone say?

But together we went, sat up front, ate popcorn and drank our Cokes together. Daddy seemed to enjoy the show but I wasn't so sure I had. Then we walked home together.

We even stopped in G'burn's, had another soft drink and listened to uncles and cousins tell stories. No one asked where we had been or anything about the court appearance. It just was not addressed even though it was certainly on my mind.

Sunday morning I got up and went to the Pentecostal Holiness Church in Hilltown as I did most Sundays. Outside, waiting for Sunday school to start, were several guys including Lonnie Burcham who was destined to become a permanent part of Hilltown when he married my cousin, Betty Jane Hill (G'burn's oldest living daughter), and settled there for the next 50 years. The Burchams lived in Fries in a company owned house, but their father was the senior deacon at the Pentecostal Church and so the entire clan of Burchams were there whenever the doors were open.

Lonnie said, "Wade, how did it go on Monday? You okay, boy?"

"Sure," I said, putting on my best front. "Went to school all week and went to the picture show last night."

By then several more guys and some girls had joined the group and were listening.

Lonnie replied, laughing softly, "I hear your daddy took you to the movies last night. And he walked you all the way home."

It was then that I realized that everyone in Hilltown knew everything, as they always did. But knowing that they knew and that they were thinking about it when I came up the road or whenever they saw me was a different type of punishment.

Judge Mathews could put me on court's probation for a limited period but that was nothing compared to everyone in Hilltown putting me on probation for good.

Lucky for me, I already had my nickname.

A Summer of Fear and Adventure

"Wade, Lois Hill has come down with polio!"

There was no question but that Momma considered this a very, very important announcement. She had her own way of making things clear.

It was around the first of July in 1950. My mother had just come into the kitchen from talking to neighbors, all relatives, in front of our house on Hilltown Road. Their conversation had been highly animated and their body language, even from a distance, demonstrated strain.

Lois Hill, Momma's cousin, lived just up the road from us with her father and mother, Dollar Bill and Stacy Hill. Lois was one of almost 200 relatives, including cousins, aunts and uncles, living in Hilltown at that time.

Lois had polio!

That declaration was enough to startle and stimulate fear in anybody in 1950. The dreaded virus usually attacked younger people in the summertime, leaving many paralyzed for life. It seemed to be running wild that summer. *The Roanoke Times* had been reporting an epidemic in nearby Wytheville where nearly 200 people, mostly children, had been sent to the Childrens' Clinic of Roanoke Memorial Hospital and diagnosed with polio.

As far as anyone knew, the first person to be diagnosed in Wytheville was the four-year-old son of a star player on the town's professional minor league baseball team. The child died, attracting widespread media attention. Suddenly, western Virginia was on the national map and there was a cloud of dread hanging over nearby communities and deep concern everywhere. When a person you knew or knew of came down with polio, that dread became very personal.

An article in *The Roanoke Times* described the reactions to the epidemic hitting so hard in Wytheville:

The streets were empty of children. Fear stalked the town. People kept to themselves. One family with a half-dozen kids dumped a load of sand in its living room so the little ones could play.... Churches cancelled services. Sunday school classes were held over the radio. Stores and theaters closed. Signs warned outsiders to stay away.

Out-of-town motorists brave enough to pass through town kept their windows rolled up, holding handkerchiefs over their faces. If they had to stop for gas, they'd crack their windows enough to shove money at the attendant, then speed away....

It was a summer of despair and panic....

And it had hit near our home—just two houses away.

Lois Hill had come down with polio!

"What?" I blurted when Momma told me of Lois' ill fortune.

I was more frightened at that moment than at any other time in my life. Polio was now just two doors away. Who would be next? Would Sister, that pretty little five-year-old blonde, get it and die, or be in an iron lung or a wheelchair or on crutches for the rest of her life?

Polio hitting so close to home changed our lives that summer and carried me and several of my Hilltown cousins into dangerous waters, literally and figuratively. Our mothers were determined to protect us and in doing so unknowingly may have exposed us to an even greater extent.

We were isolated, forbidden to play with other children, although we were allowed to leave the house to play alone in the fields and woods. (A friend later in life, C. T. Mitchell, told me of his experiences in nearby West Virginia when he was not allowed to go to the movies or to church or to ballgames where he might mingle with others his age but was allowed to work at the family grocery store as usual.) The assumption was that children caught it from one another, which may or may not have been true.

Despite the best efforts of our parents, several children of Hilltown, all cousins, often gathered at the New River that hot, muggy summer and mingled freely in and out of the low, sluggish stream and had great fun. It probably was the worst thing we could have done.

Eight-year-old Lois Hill had attended Fries School the previous fall in the first grade. She was energetic, very bright and the apple of her daddy's eye. Now she was facing a very uncertain future. In years to come, she and her wheelchair would carpool to school with my sister. Momma would deliver the two girls to school each morning and Lois' dad Dollar Bill would pick them up after school.

Many children with polio were being confined to what were called iron lungs, sometimes for life, as their lungs became paralyzed and the iron, cigar shaped tube in which their bodies were placed pumped air in and out of their failed lungs. Others, their legs paralyzed, would never walk again. And some did not survive at all.

The entire nation was at risk that summer. It seemed that the very young and people in their 20s were most likely to die, while older children and teenagers faced paralysis or lung failure. Polio seemingly did not often attack older people or if it did the effect was so mild as to not be apparent.

Americans were well aware of polio long before 1950. Although many of his countrymen did not realize it, President Franklin D. Roosevelt (1933-1945) was unable to use his legs, having been stricken with polio in 1921. I knew about polio because of my interest in the news and my Daddy's commitment to the national campaign, The March of Dimes, which raised money to assist polio patients and for research.

It seemed that every year my dad was carrying those little pasteboard cards with built in slots for 10 dimes as he asked everyone he ran into for a donation. The March of Dimes was the most successfully focused fundraising effort in history, raising some $31 million dollars in 1949 alone for polio research.

That research paid off in 1955 when a killed virus vaccine developed by Dr. Jonas Salk was declared safe and effective, triggering mass immunizations in this country and around the globe. Then, in 1961 an oral live virus vaccine developed by Dr. Albert Sabin was licensed. The new vaccines stopped polio in its tracks.

But, all that came too late for Lois Hill and thousands of American children that summer if 1950. Lois did recover and in spite of a lifelong handicap went on to attend college, marry, raise a family and live the American dream.

After a somber dinner that evening, Momma and Daddy went

to the front yard and sat in home made wooden chairs under the young maple tree and talked for a long time. Five-year-old Mickey played with toys and I was left to entertain myself watching early evening television. We had gotten the first television in all Hilltown the previous fall. After Daddy had repeatedly denounced the evil of the thing for months he had suddenly brought one home in the trunk of his car.

About 8 o'clock Momma and Daddy left their chairs under the maple tree and called Sister and me to the dining room table for a family meeting. This was something of a first and we knew it was an important occasion.

"Well, Forest and I have been talking," Daddy said. "You know that Lois came down with polio. We're scared that it's spreading."

Momma chimed in, "Everybody says you can catch it from each other. And we know that it is worse during July and August when it's hot. We've heard of more than 10 kids between here and Galax who've come down with it already. And in Wytheville, it's spreading all over," she added. "We read it in the paper."

Sister and I were already aware of the outbreak because of television and everybody talking about it all the time. We didn't have to be convinced.

"We don't want either of you playing with any other kids the rest of the summer," Daddy continued. "We won't be going to the carnival over in Galax in August and you can't go to church," he said, looking at me. I usually went to the nearby Pentecostal Holiness Church with friends every Sunday while Momma and Sister went to the Grace Baptist in Hawkstown.

"Your sister will go and spend some of the days with Granny Gilley when "Teek" isn't there," Daddy said. Teek was our first cousin, Rube's boy. "And Wade, we're depending on you staying right here and not doing anything with anybody all day long. Your Momma and I have things to do and we'll trust you to mind like we tell you."

"All day long? Every day?"

"Yep," he said, "'til after Labor Day when school will start—if they don't delay it this year." In fact, that year school was delayed until way into September.

Wow! The rest of July and all of August with nothing, absolutely nothing to do. The rest of summer league baseball had been cancelled and the swimming pool at the Fries YMCA was closed for the rest of summer. As far as the children were concerned, the whole town was shutting down.

I could read the newspaper—actually the sports section. The major league baseball games would be broadcast and I could listen to them in the afternoons. But what else could I do on those hot and muggy days of summer in the southern Appalachian Mountains?

As we were talking about what we could do to kill the time Daddy had an idea. "Wade, the blackberries are getting ripe so you can go every morning and pick the bucket full of berries for your momma for canning." Our house was on a 10-acre farm that backed up to the larger farm owned by the Huldy and Leff Carico, who were relatives by marriage. Huldy was Grandpa Windy's sister, their farm stretched down the New River behind our house.

Once aggressively farmed, these acres of rolling hills were now used as pasture land with limited attention other than fencing and some corn fields on the tops of a few ridges. As a result, clusters of blackberry vines had grown up all over the hollers and along the fence rows, making for rich pickings.

Momma usually stopped when she had canned about a hundred quarts so I had some work cut out for me. Still, that would leave plenty of free time for an active twelve year-old. How was I going to use it?

There would be no socializing with cousins, friends and playmates, no playing YMCA or country league baseball, no going down to the Fries ballpark and seeing the semipro team play under the lights. No going to Winston Salem or Chilhowie or Iron Ridge to visit a couple of days and nights with cousins. Everything was coming to a halt. It was going to be a boring summer as we hunkered down, hoping for the polio to pass over us.

Suddenly I had an idea. "Daddy, can I go down to the river?"

He seemed surprised. "Well, I don't know about that, Wade. What do you mean?"

"Can I go down to the river and pass some time fishing and

things? That is, after I've done all my chores and picked the blackberries."

He thought for a few moments, puffing on his Camel. "Well, I would guess so."

Momma jumped in, "Do any of the other boys go down there?"

"No, not in August. It's hot and kinfolks are visiting. I'd just like to walk down there and fish some. I've been down there a hundred times. Daddy you know that."

The stretch of New River behind our house was a quiet, isolated place.

"Well, if you promise you'll get your chores done first and you'll be careful down there, I guess it'll be okay. But just don't you go up the railroad to Fries or some other place where there are other kids playing. Don't you just happen to show up in some Hawkstown service station playing pinball or something else either."

"Sure," I declared happily.

"I don't even think you should be going over to your uncle Ruff Dillon's on Chestnut Creek even though his children are grown or gone for the summer." Daddy added.

"Oh, I wouldn't do that, that's too far away. I'd have to cross over Fries Junction to do that."

Sister and I went upstairs to bed but Momma and Daddy went back out under the maple tree and talked way past dark. They were worried. We were worried, too, but we tended to forget.

It took about a week to work through all the things that Momma and Daddy came up with for me to do, but by mid-July all that was left was to feed and milk the cow, mow the lawn and pick a bucket full of blackberries each day, all of which I usually completed by lunch time. The afternoons were all mine.

The first day or so I was satisfied with listening to Dizzy Dean announcing the baseball game of the day over WBOB, the Galax radio station but with my Boston Braves doing poorly again that summer the radio became boring. So I finally ventured down to the river.

The first day it took me about two hours to get to the river and explore the water and rapids. I jumped on and over rocks to reach a tiny island near the middle of the river at the beginning of the Double Shoals without getting wet. There I enjoyed the sun and breeze, dangling my feet in the water until the sun began to dip behind the towering, pine tree covered bluff that framed the river gorge. It was time to head home to milk the cow and get ready for supper.

As the days passed I began taking walks along the railroad tracks beside the river toward Fries Junction. Things new one day became boring in the next, causing me to push on and on. Fries Junction was where the railroad track coming from Pulaski forked with one line going south over the river to Galax with the other line continuing west into Fries. The train typically made two daily runs up to Fries and a secondary trip to Galax. The cotton mill at Fries relied more on the railroad than did the Galax furniture factories, which were linked to the Carolinas by highway.

The first time I wandered onto the diesel fuel-soaked trestle to look down at the river shoals I was startled by the train whistle. There was the locomotive, coming hard at me. Panicking, I turned and ran. But 20 feet from the other side, my foot got jammed between the cross ties. I jerked my foot out of my shoe made it to the other side—barely. (Pun intended.) As the coal-fired steam engine chugged past, the fireman shook his fist at me. I couldn't hear his words but since my daddy had once been a fireman and a train engineer I suspected that what he was saying was not nice.

It took me about two hours to crawl down under the trestle and fish my shoe off the concrete pier. My lesson learned, I looked around for better escape routes for future reference.

The next time I went to the junction I was again standing midway on the bridge across New River when I was surprised by a train as it backed down the tracks from Fries on its way to Galax. I had again been so preoccupied with the river and the rushing waters that the train slipped up on me. As before, my first thought was to run to the other side and beat the train. On second thought and remembering my earlier experience, I stopped in mid-span at a platform or wooden observation ledge that jutted out over the river where I could stand clear of the tracks.

As the train went chugging by at about 20 miles an hour, I was stunned to look up at the red caboose and see several guys from Hilltown and Fries—cousins all. Somehow and somewhere they had gotten on the train and were riding it to Galax. Throwing caution to the wind, I ran after the train and was able to grab the handrail leading up the steps to the rear platform of the caboose and there joined my cousins. I totally forgot the promises to Daddy and Momma and the threat of polio. These were friends and it was fun!

As the train chugged on I peered into the caboose and saw that it was empty. The Pulaski to Fries train did not merit a conductor and the fireman doubled as a brakeman, resulting in a two man crew—much to the chagrin of the Railroad Workers Union of which my grandfather Hill and several of his sons and other relatives were members. The railroad was trimming costs and short runs were being operated with skeleton crews in those days of "Ike-a-nomics" as my daddy would characterize things.

This meant we had free run of the caboose—if we didn't get caught. The ride became an almost-daily regular outing followed with a swim in the river. It was exciting and we weren't bothering anybody or worrying our parents.

It took some doing to hop off the rear of the train and back on again for the return ride but that challenge was a big part of the fun. The passenger car was still part of the train and we made sure we didn't set off any alarms. Six or seven of us enjoyed the adventure practically every day for more than two weeks.

Then one day while we were planning our exit from the train at the Chestnut Creek stop (the train stopped when there were paying passengers getting off at one of the drop-off and pickup points along the way to Galax) only to find a man in a suit and tie waiting for us as we dropped off and entered the train stop shelter. Ne-nee muttered under his breath, "Damned railroad detective!"

He took the name of everybody except Dirty who by some instinct had dropped off the train on the other side and remained out of sight. Grandpa Windy, who in 1950 had worked on the railroad almost 50 years and was ready to retire, got a letter about Ne-nee, who lived with him, and another he handed to Daddy, a former N&W worker himself. They knew.

For some reason it wasn't considered a big deal. We were not confronted and the opportunity for confession was not provided. But I sensed that somehow Momma knew. She would make little insightful remarks about catching the train at Fries Junction, both of us knowing well she had never done that and wouldn't if she could. So she must have known and given me those hints just to let me know that she knew. It wasn't like her to let it pass, but she did.

While these exciting and carefree experiences were a wonderful alternative to the usual summer activities in the mountains, we had ignored the risk of the disease, not to mention the danger of "hoboing" on the train day after day. (A hobo is a tramp or vagrant. During the Depression in the 1930s, hobos were a familiar part of American life and a headache to the railroads as they slipped aboard trains to get from one place to the next. It was said that one of my uncles had hoboed from coast to coast before coming home and settling down in the mid-1930s.)

The polio epidemic broke at the end of the summer, school started, even though a little late, and the New York Yankees beat the Philadelphia Phillies in the World Series. Life returned to normal. Our parents never realized that by granting us permission to visit the river they had inadvertently placed seven boys in grave danger.

Not all sewage was treated before it reached creeks and streams that emptied into the New River. And while Fries did have a sewage treatment plant it was primary in nature and did not attempt to attack the biological impurities which were a natural breeding medium for microorganisms such as the polio virus.

Looking back to that summer I realize it was one of great adventure when I came to know my river—the New River—better than ever.

I am glad though that Momma never openly knew. She surely would have used the opportunity as one of her examples of how one takes life and the future into his own hands by taking such risks. She could only hint that she knew. I suspected that she was just thankful to get her family through that crisis and there was no reason to second guess anyone.

Then one cool October evening sitting on our front porch seemingly staring at nothing, Momma said as if to herself, "I'm glad that summer is over."

It had been a summer to remember, nonetheless.

What Do You Want To Be?

The dapper man walked up to our car and said, "Hi Woody."
 Daddy said, "Hey Dollar."
 Shortly after a few pleasantries with Daddy, the man turned to me as I sat on the left fender of my daddy's 1930s Ford coupe, and said, "Wade boy, just what do you want to be when you grow up?"
 What did I want to be as a grown up? A question usually asked of boys in those days—but of a five year-old? I didn't have an inkling of what he was asking.
 My daddy quickly and definitively answered for me, "Wade's going to be a Civil Engineer."
 Sixteen years later, in December of 1958, I sat in the registrar's office at VPI (Virginia Polytechnic Institute then and Virginia Tech today) as Miss Clarice Slusher, the registrar, posed the same question, "Wade, what do you want to major in?"
 After pausing for a moment I said, "Well, I think it'll be Civil Engineering."
 It was a long journey from the grounds of the Mount Olive Methodist Church in June of 1942 to the decision to major in civil engineering at VPI. Especially since my father and I had never, ever had a discussion on the subject of my college major in any shape, form or fashion since the day in 1942. (Later we would talk about it, but that was after I had earned three degrees in civil engineering.) All of his suggestions and ambitions for me were indirect and occurred during conversations I overheard. Daddy never told me directly that he wanted me to go to college.

He never suggested a college that I might attend or what subject I might study in college.

However, I knew that he (and Momma, too) expected that I would go to college because of the numerous times early in my life, from the age of four to twelve, he would say to a neighbor, relative or friend in my presence, "Wade is going to college." Only that one time do I remember his mentioning the words civil engineering to me directly or indirectly.

This seems to demonstrate the enormous power of parental persuasion when articulated in terms of expectations at so young an age. His statement combined with his love for building things left a permanent imprint on my brain that would ultimately be lived out.

But first let us return to 1942.

That Sunday in June at the Mount Olive Methodist Church was Decoration Day, and all of us were dressed in our Sunday best. My daddy was wearing his best coat and tie and a wide brimmed white hat. Lawrence Hill, known as Dollar Bill or just Dollar, was also dressed in a suit, complete with vest, a fancy necktie and a light brown small brimmed hat or ivy cap placed on the side of his head. Dollar was dressed as many of the Hill men dressed for such special occasions—looking back it almost seems as if they were dressing beyond their means.

Daddy never cottoned to vests and Ivy Caps, but he was wearing his best, and perhaps only, suit. I also was wearing a new white shirt, knee length brown pants with matching jacket and a light brown small brimmed hat similar to Dollar's.

Decoration Sunday was an annual event when members of the Hill family from all across the country would come home to Hilltown and the Mount Olive Church bringing flowers for graves to honor the many ancestors and relatives who were interred there. Many attended church service on that Sunday, while others came to visit the graves, have dinner on the grounds and spend hours renewing old friendships and catching up on relatives from near and far.

Like most of the others, Daddy pulled his automobile up onto the grass, opened the trunk, took out quilts and spread them on the ground along with the many special dishes of food Momma had prepared for the day. There were many other cars with their trunks open, and food was laid out as family members wandered from site to site, munching food and enjoying conversation with others as they walked from car to car.

Momma was engaged in this visiting while Daddy and I manned our fort. Dollar walked up as we were eating fried chicken and began talking with us. I was sitting on the car fender and Daddy was leaning against the open car door.

As I would later learn, Dollar was both a skilled craftsman and cautious businessman. He was always probing for answers to questions. Being the professional automobile mechanic in the Hill family, he had sharpened his business skills, quickly learning that it was best to establish the price for services or for an item up front rather than have a prolonged discussion about it later. This was especially true if business was with kinfolks. The Hill's were noted for taking exception to things, especially where money was involved.

He became so businesslike in his demeanor that the family gave him the nickname "Dollar Bill." To some, or even most, this was a signal to not expect free services just because was a relative. Many smirked a little at times while using his nickname, indicating that he was only interested in how much money he could make but Dollar knew if he didn't draw a line there would be no end to it. He was right too.

Dollar worked as the chief automobile mechanic at the Washington Mills garage in Fries and was known to do work at home on the weekend if the time was available and the pay was right. He was the son of Jim Hill and grandson of Hilltown founder John R. Hill, and was known for the size of his land holdings (about ten or fifteen acres), the quality and size of his house, and the automobiles he drove—not fancy but obviously well cared for. He was my mother's first cousin and my first cousin once removed.

In 1942, Dollar had no children, but within a year or so a daughter was born to him and his wife Stacy. His daughter, Lois, as earlier discussed contracted polio during the epidemic of the mid 1950s and was partially paralyzed for life. However, Lois was a determined female who later attended college, had a career and a family.

As with his adult relatives, Dollar's casual conversation with me quickly turned to business—or what were my plans for life. Of course, my career plans at age four were less than certain and I could not have answered such a question if given the opportunity.

With no chance given, my daddy had stepped in and answered for me. I had no idea at that time what it meant to be a civil engineer. However, I now know that my daddy was articulating his own unmet goals. He had dreamed of going to college and being a basketball player and becoming a civil engineer. He was dealt a fatal blow to achieving this dream when his father died of spinal meningitis just as Daddy was in the middle of his senior year in high school in Smyth County, Virginia. The principal there had identified Charles Woodrow Gilley as college material and had been working to get him a scholarship at nearby Emory and Henry College. Unfortunately, at age nineteen my daddy had become the sole breadwinner for his mother and six younger brothers and sisters, effectively ending his college dreams.

He worked in and out of the construction business most of his life as a carpenter and a brick mason with occasional forays into the home building business. His last home construction project came in 1978 after retiring from the Hercules Powder Company in Radford Virginia, when he and his friends finished a summer home my wife and I had started in Bland County, Virginia on some eighty nine acres on the Wilderness Road adjoining the Jefferson National Forest.

Thus, it would be years later that I would recall these comments and came to realize that in answering Dollar's question Daddy was in reality articulating his own unrealized ambitions. Most amazing to me is that he never again mentioned this desire, for me or for himself. But obviously it was an idea planted that later grew to full fruition.

All during my early high school years, I worked on home building projects for Daddy as he continued to build ranch style homes everywhere we lived. He loved to work with his hands and see useful projects finished. I'll always remember a set of builder's books he kept for decades, including one that dealt primarily with trigonometry.

I worked on highway construction projects two summers before going away to college in the fall of 1957, and though he'd passed his knack of construction on to me, he was always better than me. I had a knack for math and science and the educational opportunities fate had denied him. But I had never used the words 'civil engineering' in relation to myself until sitting across the desk from Miss Slusher at the end of the fall quarter in 1958.

Actually, I had entered VPI in the fall of 1957 with only one intention—that of playing football for Frank O. Moseley. And I did practice under him for two fall and one spring sessions before coming to the conclusion that I would not make a living playing ball. In fact, I would never play ball for VPI. I practiced with the freshman football team in the fall of 1957 and was on the freshman wrestling team. I practiced with Bill Redd's baseball team the following spring along with spring football practice, but never played a game in either sport. In the fall of 1958, I decided to look for other options.

After talking with Coach Moseley, I ended up in Miss Slusher's office hoping to get admitted to a specific degree-granting program.

I had enrolled in pre-engineering (in something of a probationary status) upon entering VPI and had struggled, due in part to my limited background at Fries High school and in part to the many hours I devoted to practicing football, baseball and wrestling as well as being a member of the required cadet program.

So, when she asked what area of engineering I might wish to major in, I had only one answer and that was my daddy's answer given that Sunday in 1942—Civil Engineering.

More than Daddy's expectations were Momma's determination that Sister and I get a good education, including going to college, which had gotten me to the point where I had to choose a major. Daddy always talked in expectations and was encouraging about college but Momma was practical. That practical side of her was manifested in many different ways over the years after Sister was born.

For example, when I entered the ninth grade she returned to work specifically to save money to send me to college. She returned to a second shift spinner's job at the cotton mill which had slowed to three days a week and brought home less than ten dollars a week after having twelve dollars set aside for my college tuition. In four years she saved some $1,300, which was enough for two full years at VPI where the tuition, room and board and laundry was $649 for a full year. While I took the first year's contribution from her (less what Granny Oda had contracted for) by the second year I had figured out how to make a contribution and in the final two years I paid the entire amount myself.

Strange as it may seem, Momma's approach to my education after Sister showed up changed from one of total domination (she had to work on Sister) to one of direction and support. For example, she insisted that my teachers were flawless, telling my second grade teacher Mrs. Jackson to "give him a paddling whenever he needs it and then send a note home and we'll give him another one," That was an extraordinary year with me getting 63 paddlings and spankings and switchings at school and three at home. (The notes got 'lost' after I put two and two together.) But as Momma most likely guessed it was a year not forgotten, and the perfect attendance and straight As were a bonus to us both.

Neither Momma nor Daddy paid much attention to the extracurricular activities I pursued in school. Neither ever saw me play a high school football, basketball or baseball game, even though I earned eleven letters, some All Star recognitions, a major sportsmanship award and a very brief tryout with—you guessed it the Milwaukee Braves. They knew though, for I was always late in getting home to milk the cow and eat dinner with Sister, as Momma was working that second shift. The only discussions I had with her in those years was in the morning when she arose early to fix my breakfast of biscuits, gravy and fatback after milking and before I dressed for school. We had little more time on weekend mornings but Saturdays were filled with catch-up work on the farm and elsewhere and Sunday was a baseball day for me.

Momma quit looking at my grade reports after returning to the mill, and while I knew her expectations, the days of all As never really returned. If fact, all through college and graduate school she just didn't seem interested in grades and such information.

There were occasions when Daddy and I had serious conversations. In fact, that fall of 1958, when I made the decision to try Civil Engineering, we spoke for more than an hour long distance about it. I had serious reservations about engineering while he was optimistic saying, "Give it a try, you can always major in business if it doesn't work out."

But one thing happened my senior year in high school which demonstrated both Momma's ingenuity and appreciations for Daddy's dream. On investigating colleges and their football teams, we found that I could easily get into places from nearby Emory and Henry College to the University of North Carolina and the University of Maryland as a football player. However, places like VPI and N. C. State, with their heavy emphasis on engineering and science, were another story. Fries High School had not offered trigonometry—a clear prerequisite for engineering.

While we were considering this dilemma, Momma left me a note one September evening in 1956 with the following, "Have you thought about Sun Rise Semester?" Those early mornings while I milked the cow she had apparently been watching television and the only thing that interested her at six in the morning (we only got two channels back then) was this televised college course by New York University called Sunrise Semester. It was something of correspondence course enhanced by a professor writing math problems on the blackboard while his back was turned to the camera.

Upon checking, I found that VPI wouldn't recognize correspondence courses or so Dr. Landon fuller said. And when Momma talked to our high school principal Mr. Ned he snorted, "high schools don't take college credit." When she pursued the question he allowed as how if I took a regular correspondence course and Miss

Smith, the school librarian and Police Chief Bruce Smith's old maid sister, monitored the tests, he would enter it on my high school transcript—if I passed. VPI said they would take it as long as it was on the Fries High School Transcript.

The end result of this collaboration between Momma, New York University, Mr. Ned, Miss Smith and VPI was, with my participation, credit (no grade) on my high school transcript for Trigonometry. I was admitted to VPI in pre-engineering and football for the fall of 1957—ready or not.

Momma apparently never doubted my ability once the course was determined. She was equally as focused on Sister. In fact, as Sister approached the end of her high school days Momma up and moved the family to Dublin, Virginia so that Sister could attend Radford College for Teachers, a branch of VPI. Momma proved that she would sacrifice anything, including leaving her Hilltown, to ensure her daughter's success and, not unlike Granny Oda, the security of a daughter's presence.

Of course, both Sister and I graduated from college and Momma achieved a primary goal of her life. That is not to say that she still did not have opinions and a willingness to share them. However, I, as previously mentioned, spent the time from the moment of leaving Hilltown in September of 1957 to the time of Momma's passing like a gerbil on a wheel, constantly fighting for better position through education. Within eight years of finishing high school late, at almost nineteen years of age, I had earned a doctorate in engineering, worked as a math and engineering professor and spent more than twenty months working in the defense industry. Now in 198,1 I was secretary of education in Virginia and Momma was ill.

My wife Nanna and I had moved thirteen times, had three children, lost a child and spent fourteen years in high level educational positions by the time Momma passed away. I later wondered about myself, what she had created, coming from a family where her father had worked for almost fifty years for the same company and a husband who had worked for one company the last twenty five years of his career.

I am sure "Sister" Mickey was more of the model she was think-

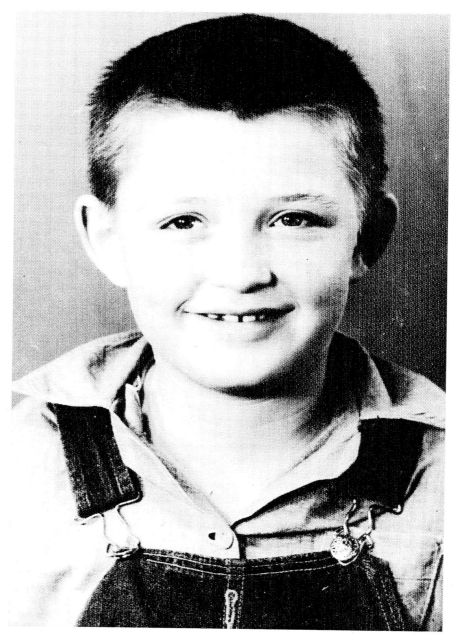

Wade Gilley gets 63 paddlings in the second grade, in 1946.

ing of: a master's degree, a school teacher, married with twin girls and living close enough for almost daily contact—not unlike Grandpa Windy and his children in another age. Momma had believed that the pursuit of a better life began and ended with education.

But at the end, she wanted one more chance for us to talk like we did Before Sister as she said, "Wade, I've wanted to talk like we did in Roanoke."

Epilogue

Standing at Momma's grave site, with Nanna and our children, Daddy, Sister and her family and lots of relatives, that Fourth of July weekend as she was lowered in to the ground beside my first daughter, I found myself returning to her last words, our last conversation. She didn't get that one last Roanoke, World War II conversation that she wanted but Momma in her own way had stepped in and caused me to rethink some things. She had a message to a forty one year-old type I diabetic workaholic.

As the funeral service ended and the family retreated I found myself beside my thirteen year-old daughter following Nanna with our son as we walked back to our car. "Cheryl," I said as we walked along, "Momma Gilley wants us to talk more."

She and Momma had been big talkers for years. Once after Momma spent a week visiting with us, seven year-old Cheryl had accompanied Momma in her car as we drove home. When we stopped for a rest after about three hours on the road I found that they had fallen out. Cheryl was pouting. Momma had said to her as they got out of the car, "For the rest of the way home let's both be real quiet." Her granddaughter had taken the suggestion personally.

Forest had found her match in the talking business. This wasn't like a son who would listen all day, if he could sit still.

"Momma Gilley wanted us to talk more and I'm going to listen to her. We need to spend some time together," I continued.

"That's okay with me Daddy," she replied.

The realization that I needed to stop and think about things led to a whole new phase of our lives. Instead of returning to a college presidency, after my term as secretary of education, I took a lower paying job as special assistant to the president of George Mason University in the Washington D. C. area. We sold our four bedroom, three bath brick home and moved into a sixteen hundred square foot three bedroom town house that required total renovation which we did ourselves, falling back on Daddy's lessons. Nanna went back to teaching, making use of her two degrees from VPI.

The great thing about this new job was the freedom it gave me. It not only provided an opportunity to learn and grow professionally, but gave me the personal time to remodel a house, take more extensive vacations with the family (and some of those have their own stories) and time to spend with the children—*talking*—as they grew up.

During the years between 1981 and 1991, I saw my daughter play scores of tennis matches in high school and in college where she captained the tennis team as she prepared for law school. During that same time frame I became a basketball freak, seeing my son play lots of games in high school as he attended a basketball oriented prep school in the Washington D. C. area. (He had four teammates who later played in the NBA.)

We took Momma up on one of her interests, traveling, with one or all journeying to Spain, France, England, Brazil, Alaska, Japan, Hawaii, China, Jamaica and other places over those years. Those were important educational experiences for us all and they have their stories too. But I doubt they were as impressive or as exciting as taking the midnight train to the Ocean View beach in 1943.

During those years we talked a lot and much of it was about Momma and Daddy and growing up in Hilltown. In a senior paper for a creative writing degree, our daughter presented the Hilltown Story in terms of the nicknames of my relatives. Her professor wrote on that paper, which she still has, "You have the makings of a book here."

And then one day, my son, who also holds an engineering degree, said, "I've heard all of those stories before. What do you plan to do with them?"

What could I do? I wondered. And then I knew.

I would write a book. Momma's story.

Appendix

Fries!

Fries, Virginia—one of America's first planned communities. Who would have thought of it that way when I was growing up?

In fact, it wasn't until the early 80s when we lived in Reston, Virginia, that I heard the words "planned community." Then I realized I had grown up near one of America's first planned communities, developed by the great planner and builder, Colonel Francis Henry Fries, who also built the industrial city of Mayodan, in North Carolina. (Fries is pronounced "freeze". People often joked that the town was named fries in the summer and freeze in the winter.) Years afterward, as a civil engineer I realized that corporate America had built many planned communities in the first half of the twentieth century, as an integral part of the evolving Industrial Age.

The town of Fries was founded as the result of an Act of Congress in 1901 and the ingenuity of Colonel Fries, a famous North Carolinian, who came to the Bartlett Falls section of the New River, in Grayson County, Virginia. His aim was to first build a hydroelectric dam to power a large textile (cotton) mill, then later a complete community. He proceeded to build the mill and the community in conjunction with construction of the dam.

By the time Colonel Fries had finished his work in Grayson County, Virginia, he had constructed a concrete and stone dam forty feet high and more than three hundred feet long, which not only powered the mill but provided all of the electricity for the new town and the entire adjacent countryside, including my home

175

community. Hilltown, founded by John R. and Martha Jane Corvin Hill in 1868, on a high plateau over looking the great bend of the ancient New River, had electricity and telephones decades before most of its sister mountain communities across western Virginia, all because of the dam built by Colonel Fries.

As he was building the dam, Fries constructed a large and complex cotton mill, which in time would accommodate more than 3,000 workers over three shifts and seven days a week—one of the first 24/7 operations we hear a lot about today. The Colonel then built a complete town that accommodated the total needs of more than 1,200 souls residing there and another 1,000 or so in the surrounding countryside needed to support the large mill complex.

Fries included a commercial and business complex that would put Wal-Mart or Sam's to shame a hundred years later. Downtown Fries boasted a major store complex that included, among others, a drug store, a grocery store, men's and women's clothing stores, a hardware store, a U.S. Post Office, doctors' and dentists' offices and a Masonic Lodge, where officials of the company were leaders for decades. Workers in the cotton mill could all have open credit accounts at any of these establishments, including the Masonic Lodge, with regular deductions coming from their weekly paychecks. Not more than twenty percent of their check could be deducted for these accounts, and there was no interest accruing.

In a similar fashion, Colonel Fries provided homes for more than a thousand people in three hundred houses of various sizes. The largest and best houses, some four and five bedrooms, were on Bosses' Row and Farmer's Circle. In other areas of the town, a half-dozen mansions were built for the executives or bosses of the mill, who all moved to Fries from one of the North Carolina operations of Washington Mill, Inc. The larger working families lived in two, three and four bedroom homes along Church Street, Main Street or Railroad Street (now named Riverview Street since it runs along an elevated ridge overlooking the train track, thus possessing a wonderful view of the New River.)

As one moved up the hillside that constituted a major part of the town of Fries in view were Boarding House Street, Second

Street, Third Street and the famous Top Street, where, it was said, one could see over the clouds on a rainy day. Farther up the hillside, the houses became smaller and smaller, with most of the Top Street houses having just three rooms and a half bath. In Fries, a mill worker could have a house to suit his family and pocket book with no one paying more than a quarter of his wages for housing.

All of the homes built by Colonel Fries had an indoor bathroom and running water, amenities not found in places like Hilltown or even larger Virginia communities until decades later. One of the first things Colonel Fries built was a water treatment plant and a sewage treatment plant, the latter being one of the first in Virginia. It was considered advanced for rural communities until after the environmental laws passed by congress in the 1970s. Communities like Richmond and Washington D.C. only decades later set in motion the environmental initiatives of the good Colonel.

But the Colonel did not stop there. He provided a complete recreational program for the town and surrounding communities by building, all shortly after the turn of the twentieth century, a super modern YMCA, which had meeting places, a library, a movie theater, a bowling alley and a billiard pool parlor. Later, just after World War II, the "Y" and the "Company" built a very modern outdoor swimming pool, which was constructed by my Daddy in his occasional role as builder and contractor. However, long before building the pool, the Company, through the auspices of the Y, built a modern baseball park with electric lights in the early 1920s. Because it was the only such facility within a hundred miles, those lights burned five and six nights a week. Not only did people play baseball there but also held football games, country music concerts and religious revivals, plus carnivals and county fairs, and other events. This lighted athletic field made the town of Fries the center of many things well into the Great Depression, when New Deal programs came along to provide electricity, recreational facilities and other amenities for other parts of rural America.

Colonel Fries was not stopping there, though. He built a modern school and later convinced the Virginia General Assembly to authorize a special school district at Fries, Virginia, separate and independent from the schools of either Carroll or Grayson Counties. In the eyes of the General Assembly and the law, Fries had city status in Virginia, even though it was officially a town. Fries schools were thought to be excellent, so much so that people moved into town just to take advantage of them. Later, residents of Carroll County on the north side of the New River petitioned for and became part of the Fries High School district rather than having to travel to Woodlawn High, way across the river (that is how Sister and I became Fries High Wildcats.) Colonel Fries (wonder builder that he was) also provided accommodations for travelers who happened to stop in the town by building and operating a hotel—the Washington Inn. Those workers who lived by themselves and had no need for a complete house were provided with boarding houses—one for men, as well as one for women, for the mill required skilled spinners and weavers, along with a substantial office work force. The cotton mill was a Mecca for single women who wanted to join the work force and sneak independence early in the century. They outnumbered the men in the 1,200 base workforce by a ratio of two to one in the 1930s. My mother, Forest Gladys Hill, dropped out of school after the seventh grade at age fifteen to work in the mill, finding those six day weeks, with ten hour days, to be both economically and personally liberating. The mill, as much as almost anything else, shaped her life.

Colonel Fries thought of the spiritual aspects of life, too, providing the land and building the first church buildings in town—a Baptist Church and a Methodist Church—which accommodated most of the religious needs of the population. There were few, if any, Catholics or Jews, and the more fervent of the religious groups, such as the Pentecostal Holiness congregation and the Hard Shell Baptists, built churches and religious communities in the surrounding areas. Colonel Fries was essentially interested in taking care of the mainstream as a part of his planned community.

And still more was provided in this planned community, which was built all at one time. The streets were laid out by engineers. There were concrete sidewalks and streetlights almost everywhere. There were police and fire departments, too, in what was the first decade of the 20th Century. The Colonel also provided for restaurants, service stations, garages, and wholesale distribution centers to service the entire region. Most important, he arranged for the Norfolk and Western to make Fries a major rail hub for southwest Virginia in exchange for a monopoly on freight and passenger service. This alone provided many jobs for the most prosperous of Hilltown and other places. Not for residents of Fries, though, where the principal breadwinner had to work for the mill to qualify for company housing.

In Fries everyone had work, and the children were provided for uniquely for that time. Many of the children had advanced education. Fries High School had a rate of more then forty percent going on to college in the mid 1950s. Discounting the community college enrollments, this would be equivalent to that of the state of Virginia at the turn of the 21st Century.

There were plenty of extra-curricular activities in Fries, also. When I was growing up, if your parents worked in the mill it cost nothing to belong to the YMCA. Otherwise, it cost one dollar per year in 1950. That included free membership in summer baseball teams and winter basketball teams, the equivalent of today's little leagues. There was basketball for girls as early as 1920, as well as tennis on the set of clay courts built before World War I. Fries had the first indoor basketball court west of Roanoke, Virginia the home of the Norfolk and Western Railroad. This covered a territory some one hundred by two hundred miles or 20,000 square miles.

Today, with the advent of NAFTA and other forces, American manufacturing has jumped the international boundaries. Places like Fries cannot sustain a competitive edge—thus, the core reason for it existence has disappeared. Yet, even today, the core elements of this planned community are retained. On return trips from time to time, I am amazed when I take stock of what was there—how forward the thinking had been more than a hundred years earlier. While Hilltown reflected the Hill culture of those Blue Ridge Mountains, something very important to me as I was growing up, Fries was an important adjunct, with a culture all its own. Hilltown shaped *the who* and Fries perhaps helped shape *the what* of young men and women growing up there between 1901 and 1957.

Momma could always get a job in the mill for she was an excellent spinner. Daddy worked for the mill in the mid 1930s and, then again, by necessity, in the late 1940s, just before getting a permanent job at the Radford Arsenal at the beginning of the Korean War in 1950. In the interim, he worked on constructing the arsenal, and for the Norfolk and Western Railway, first as a fireman, and then an engineer. After the war he made several attempts to go into business for himself. He was a very capable man who was just not built for managing business and money. If he had only let Momma handle the money, it is hard to tell how successful his trucking or construction businesses could have been.

It would have appeared to a Fries-ite that Woodrow Gilley spent a lot of time and effort avoiding working at the mill. That might have put some company people off. In its early years, the cotton mill and town had excellent leadership in people like Jack Thorpe, who ran things for a quarter of a century. In time, with the changing global economy the vision of people like Colonel Fries and John Thorpe was no longer the controlling or driving force. The mill gradually declined and closed in the 1980s. Fries is now not the growing, unique place it once was but it remains a unique place for both current residents and those of us who look back with positive memories.

I remember a town and community that Francis Fries and John Thorpe created, one that was largely in place according to their vision during the period of my own maturing. Simply put, I was fortunate to have had the opportunity to grow up in Hilltown and Fries. Like Hilltown, Fries was a remarkable place at a unique time in the history of America. It is an integral part of this story—Before Sister... in Hilltown.

Note: Colonel Francis Henry Fries was obviously a very talented and visionary man. Before building the cotton mill at Bartlett Falls on the New River and the town of Fries, Colonel Fries was on a path with destiny. His family owned a major textile empire in North Carolina, and in the late 1800s the Colonel teamed with Richard J. Reynolds, a tobacco warehouseman (R.J. Reynolds— remember that name?) originally from Patrick County, Virginia, and others to build a railroad from Roanoke, Virginia to Winston Salem, North Carolina. It was later sold to the Norfolk and Western Railroad. During that venture he discovered falls on the Mayo River, sufficient to build a dam, a mill and a town— Mayodan, N. C., which was finished in about 1896. Francis H. Fries founded and served as the first president of Wachovia Bank, which grew into a large national bank and survived into the 21st Century. He is credited with founding the Winston Salem Foundation in 1919.

One could write a complete book on the life and accomplishments of Colonel Fries, and I suspect others have, but suffice it to say, he was an extraordinary man. The town named for him celebrated its one-hundredth birthday in 2002.